Chaos Curse – Souls Within

The Devil Inside

- Saga II: Hellgate Frenzy: Book 1: -

Story & Cover
By
Michael Anderson

: Vol: 1
THE MAN WITH CRIMSON EYES

Disclaimer:

All characters, names, events, etc., are all works of fiction and any similarities to real life are purely coincidence. This book contains graphic scenes of violence, blood and gore, use of alcohol, discrimination, and other instances of material that may be found offensive to some. They are not the view or opinion of the author in any way, shape, or form, but instead, are used to emphasize the dark world that the story takes place in.

ISBN-13: 978-1717015617
ISBN-10: 1717015611

TO CONTACT THE AUTHOR
Please send an email to the following address...
MichaelAnderson89@mail.com

1st Edition

DEDICATED TO:

My grandfather, Andy Anderson, a grumpy old man who told you like it was. In reality, he was a guy who cared too much. Throughout my life, he helped me in more ways than I can count. He is without a doubt one of the people who made me who I am today.

May he rest in peace.

TABLE OF CONTENTS:

PROLOGUE
DOWN WITH THE SICKNESS

September 2nd, 2006

There is an explosion in the Nevada desert.

September 3rd,

Local authorities investigate the scene. The U.S. Military arrives as dawn breaks and locks down the location. Investigating reveals the remains of a secret facility impacted by an asteroid. The former of which is withheld from the public. They tell the people an asteroid hit a natural gas pocket underground on impact.

January 6th, 2007

Six months later, there is another incident five miles southeast. In the town of Parish Falls, a vulture attacks a farmer. He survives the attack and guns down the bird. Animal control collects the carcass. Later that day, for no reason, the farmer goes on a killing spree and takes the lives of eight people. The small town is horrified.

January 7th,

Upon examination of the vulture's remains, an unrecorded virus is discovered. The CDC is informed.

January 8th,

Within twenty-four hours, the CDC finds a hostile virus of which the likes had never been seen before. The CDC creates a quarantine zone around Parish Falls and tests the citizens.

Elsewhere, Reporter Samantha Grimm arrives to interview the farmer, now held in the state penitentiary. Shortly after they start, the seemingly regretful farmer begins acting strangely. He becomes violent as his veins turn black. After effortlessly breaking free of his restraints, he kills Samantha and her cameraman on live television.

As the camera continues to broadcast, the nation witnesses Samantha revive with the same black veins. One by one, the victims rise and their numbers grow. The town is lost within the day.

January 9th,

The government sends a team to investigate. They are all killed, but not before sending back video evidence of the outbreak. The U.S. panics and carpet bombs the area.

January 10th,

The CDC quarantines the ruins of the city and establishes the Parish Falls Research Base. Victims are found with a strange black substance running through their veins. This information leaks, but the government denounces the claims.

Conspiracy theories spread, and the internet tries to connect it back to the Nevada Desert incident with baseless facts and wild conjecture. Rumors of government testing run rampant, and the meteor impact is called a lie and dubbed The Event by the internet.

January 14th,

The city of Bat Cove, ten miles away was infected and subsequently razed by the U.S. military. Researchers find no apparent connection linking the two incidents.

January 16th,

The recently created Parish Falls research base is found ravaged by the infected. Simultaneously, neighboring cities report a strange black liquid running through their natural water. Hours later, these cities go dark and are found overrun with infected. The CDC releases a press announcement warning citizens of the dark water. A state of emergency is issued for Nevada.

January 20th,

It is discovered that the newly coined Darkwater has been spreading underground. A clear line of origin is connected directly back to Parish Falls, and to the epicenter of the Event. Critics slam the CDC, saying that their so-called data seems to suggest that Darkwater is spreading in an almost lifelike manner. Rather than spreading outward, it is moving directly toward populated areas. American citizens verbally attack the government.

January 23rd,

A national task force is put together from multiple agencies, and an extensive operation begins. Nevada is evacuated, and walls are put up as they begin purifying the infected areas.

February 4th,

"Crisis Averted" the government proclaims and the country rejoices. Almost like an ill-omen, a dark storm system forms on the horizon, a foreboding darkness. Despair comes crushing as the storm pours a black stained rain. One-fourth of Nevada is lost in an instant. The Darkwater had been transmitted through the natural water cycle.

February 8th,

The storm over Nevada continues to grow in size, raining Darkwater across the west coast. The Darkwater spreads like wildfire, consuming the U.S. in days. Once the Darkwater hits the ocean, it consumes the world in weeks. The storm becomes a super system, covering the entire world, and global communication is lost due to interference.

Meanwhile, the infected feed with a blind need as they become faster and stronger. With each passing wave, those infected turn quicker. God-fearing individuals begin calling it Revelations, the end times, thus coining the name, Revelation Virus.

February 12th,

Whispers speak of those who fall into comas instead of becoming infected, only to never wake up. The people pray for a cure.

February 20th,

The failing U.S. government puts together one last fighting force: the RSE, the Revelation Survival Effort. This group meets with little success and quickly devolves into old soldiers and fanatics training new meat for the grinder. Anyone seasoned enough to fight had long since died on the front lines. What started as an organized, official force became a ragtag group of inexperienced soldiers. Despite their valiant effort, they were all but forgotten overnight.

March 3rd,

Time begins slipping for the people, the days had begun to blur together.

Date Unknown,

The infected weaken, they rot away into withered shells and are called Husks. Even with brittle bodies, Husks retain their enhanced physical strength.

This sudden change spurs the people into action and breathes new life into the RSE. With the people united behind a common goal, the tides turn, and the RSE earns massive support. The war is won!

The Husks begin to thin quickly, too quickly. Then more powerful Husks appear. Overnight, they change, and so do the rules. This rapid evolution is unnatural, and they begin to mutate exponentially. Many variants rise, giving birth to the species known as the Fallen. These new beasts are unharmed by even the most powerful of human weapons.

Humans are faced with creatures seen only in horror movies. The Widowmaker, a deadly female beauty with claws that can cut steel. The Longman, a tall, grey, slender male figure devoid of defining characteristics. The Bulge, an amorphous blob of flesh and guts. Each day seemed to bring new terrors, with more powerful creatures forming from the combination of multiple Husks.

The RSE becomes beaten and broken.

Reports of a single Widowmaker wandering onto a base circulate. Bullets, knives, and explosions don't slow it down. They say in the dark of night, you can still hear if wailing from under the tank they dropped on it.

All seems hopeless, the virus spreads faster than ever. Soon, it jumps to insects, plants, and other life forms.

The wilderness becomes a harsh environment and is known to the people as the Abyss.

Within a world of death, humanity crumbles. Sixty percent of the human race has either died or become Fallen. In humanity's darkest hour, the world itself grew even darker.

Once again, whispers of those who fell into comas spread again. Those who fell into a death-like hibernation began to awaken. At first, they seemed fine, if a little different.

They say it started with a man. The Fallen attacked, and something snapped inside him. He raised his hand, and what jumped forth was a flame that incinerated the beast. Monsters that couldn't be harmed by even the likes of bombs were burned to ashes. This man became legend.

Soon, stories of others with godlike powers emerged. They spoke of a woman who could liquefy a being's bones and pull it from their bodies like water with her mind. A man who secreted acid from his pores that could dissolve anything. A mysterious human that could make any matter so soft that it could be eaten like a marshmallow. Even stories of someone whose body mimicked any material it touched.

These people became known as Sleepers, and they were gods. Each one of these superhumans had a power, and they were the only things that could hurt the Fallen. It was like God had handed down the very tools humanity needed to survive. The people formed tribes around these chosen ones.

However, these saviors quickly became their slavers. Many theories spread, but no one knew. Was it mental illness brought on by the virus or the strain of having powers? Did the lack of any who would challenge their authority corrupt them? Had the Fallen evolved to look human?

These monsters raped, murdered, and tortured the people. They began killing faster than the Fallen could. If a thought crossed their minds, there was no filter to keep them from enacting it.

It is estimated that the Sleepers alone destroyed another 10% of the human population. Among these monsters, seven terrible and fearsome monsters appeared with powers unlike any other. Each of them earned the title of an Omega by destroying an entire city single-handedly, and they became boogeymen to even the most hardened of soldiers. The Fallen avoided these demons, so society was left with a choice. Wander the Abyss and die a quick, painful death only to rise as a Fallen and kill their loved ones, or die a slow and agonizing death as a Sleeper's play toy.

People always tend to pick the more painful option out of fear. So, they huddled around the Sleepers to survive.

May 28th, 2007

That fateful day the earth rumbled and the sky roared. On every horizon, a radiant, golden light cascaded out as if pouring down from the heavens. When it faded, beacons of light shone brightly. The people were drawn to them and found solace within mysterious golden barriers. It was discovered the infected couldn't pass through.

The streams that ran black with Darkwater were filtered, letting clean water flow through. No longer could the Abyss hurt them, nor its occupants harm them. The people called these wondrous barriers Hellgates, for they kept out the hellish nightmare. However, there was only one remaining issue. The Sleepers that had used them for amusement could also pass through the Hellgates. The RSE was no more, and from its remains rose a new organization: the SAS, the Sleeper Annihilation Service.

Humanity felt that they should thank the Sleepers for their "hospitality", in kind...

CHAPTER 0
RUDE AWAKENING

The silence of the night and the beauty of the stars were almost calming as I lay bleeding. I screamed in pain as I squeezed the desert sand through my fingers. Wounds lined my body like cracks in glass, some bone-deep, and my face twisted in rage and insanity. With a deep breath, I used my legs to thrust myself to my feet and stumbled incoherently. Having regained my balance, I rushed forward with my fists readied.

A pillar of flame stretched across the horizon like a beam and stopped against my bare hands. With the back of my hands pressed together, I dug my fingers into the fire and ripped it asunder. As the flames dissipated, a man cloaked in the same fire struck my jaw and forced me to my knee. Pain invaded my body, but the flames left no mark. Despite the agony, I grabbed his fist through the fire as I sank my fingers into his skin.

Malice, concentrated hatred and murderous intent surged from the fingertips of my free hand in the form of red electricity. I clenched those fingers into a fist and struck his jaw with my hate. A red wave of energy cascaded over his face and electrical arcs danced upon him, cutting his flesh like razors. The mysterious figure stumbled back as he spit out blood, and wiped it away with a smirk. A tuft of red hair fell into view through a slice in the hood of his black trench coat. He enjoyed the fight too much to care about his own pain as he put his fist into my side. My ribs absorbed all the force they could before they gave in.

Malice reverberated through my veins like an echo, and my eyes glowed red as my muscles fed off the pain. Pain always causes hate. This hatred left a void as my darkness waned, and I felt the pressure of a foreign energy swell deep within. The vacuum flooded with ethereal energy, and my irises burned as they split. Above and below my pupils, blue energy fanned open and formed something akin to an hourglass shape. Red and blue fought like two warring powers. Suddenly, the same blue light radiated from my ribs as they snapped back in place and pushed his fist away.

The man leaped back and gathered fire between his hands, and a volley of fireballs jumped from the flames like machine gun fire. My body became less responsive with each step I took to evade. Every hit flooded me with pain but left me unscathed. He used the opening to plant his knee in my gut, and I coughed up blood.

My legs were swept from under me with a single kick. He jumped on top of me and pummeled my face with his flaming fists. With every punch, malice coursed through my entire being. He rolled away before I countered, which allowed me time to stand. I lunged forward, full of bloodlust as a burning rage exploded from within me. I needed to kill, but I could muster no more than a limp punch. I was brushed aside like a child and quickly punched in the nose, jabbed in the jaw, and elbowed on top of my head.

The red in my eyes glowed brightly, like a demon peering through the darkness. I strained against the man's elbow with nothing more than willpower. I broke free and pushed the crown of my skull into his face. He stumbled from my barrage of attacks before he tripped. I disappeared from his sight and faded into the night before I appeared over him, looming like Death's scythe.

There was no time to react, and his nose broke against my forehead. Without a twitch, he slammed his palm into my chest. An explosion erupted on contact, and I was sent soaring back into the sand. I writhed in pain as he returned to his feet with his hands held high as he gathered fire above. The flame grew with a life of its own until it was larger than him.

My body was too spent to stand, he had won. I fruitlessly kicked like a robotic toy that had fallen over. As the man threw the massive ball of fire as I continued to flail in the sand like a pathetic animal. The fire crashed down over me and engulfed my last flicker of hope. My eyes reacted to the light of the flames, and my pupils shrank almost as if to guard against it.

Then the whispers of a quiet voice echoed through my head. The voice cried out in desperation as it tried to reach me. The last of my strength faded, and I fell into darkness. A weight was lifted, and it raised me higher. I finally heard the voice, and it screamed one word, "FIGHT!!!"

My eyes opened wide, and my pupils expanded. With a twisted grin, my eyes shook violently as the blue hourglass in them spread open like wings. They violently rattled like the chains of a monster's cage as it clawed its way out. My eyes shone like the afternoon sky, and light projected from them as ethereal energy spread down my right arm. It wrapped around it and lifted me like a puppet.

With a mind of its own, it dragged me upright to stop the fireball. Darkness, blacker than the night flowed from my fingertips and became a barricade that repelled the flames. The man pushed them harder with his will, but my other arm sprang to life to reinforce the shield. With the fury of the fire that fought against me, I stood higher as I dug my feet into the sand. With one final push, it was no longer able to bend my will, and my soul forged into steel.

I fed the shield more power, and let it grow as his flames powered up in return. We waged war like wild animals who refused to back down, but soon the darkness gave. Darkness wasn't meant to shield, it could no longer take the force, and cracked as white energy slipped through. The darkness shattered, and in its death sparked a shield of white light. Where the darkness had failed, the light overtook the flames.

With a flick of my wrist, the shield launched it like the pathetic ember it was. Once it was in orbit, the light shattered, and I fell to my knees. I placed one foot forward to stand as malice flowed from me like red steam. The man snapped his fingers, sparked a ball of fire, and threw it with no effort. On instinct, I crushed the fire in my hand as I stared at the sand beneath and laughed.

I looked up, eyes red as my hair turned pitch black, and grinned like a devil. Then my eyes pulsed blue, a beacon, a herald to the soul within as it broke from its chains. My hair flashed in rhythm with my irises, becoming phosphorescent and white at the peak of the surge before it faded back to black. It swayed in the windless air as my body burned from the inside out. Single strands of hair remained white with each passing wave of energy.

Suddenly, the flame thought extinguished by my grasp erupted between my fingers and slithered up my arm like a snake. As the fire spread, my flesh burned like coal, but my hand was unscorched. Like a burning halo, from my shoulder, it spread across my scarred chest, but never up my neck. It wrapped around my torso, stopped at my waist, and ended at my opposite wrist before it fizzled out. The flames stopped as if their hunger had been satiated.

I remained unharmed by the flames as I rose. As I stood in the moonlight, my burnt flesh split down my chest. It fell open like a jacket and revealed the smooth skin beneath. A surge of power flooded through me as the jacket cracked with a red-orange glow that shone through like lava. Once the cracks overtook the jacket, my hair burst with energy. It became rock hard as a cloud of glowing dust faded around me.

With a final push, energy in the shape of white, constantly shifting fur erupted from my collar and wrists. My sick grin was an unsettling sight and meant the fight was far from done…

CHAPTER 1
THE WORLD WE LIVE IN

OVER THE CRYSTAL HAVEN HELLGATE, AUGUST 27TH, 2007 -- On a dark, stormy night, a plane flew through a turbulent sky. A young boy and his small sister lay hidden from sight.

We were getting a new life, my sister and I, or we hoped. Soon, we'd be in Clearcrest, a city in the ruins of New York protected by the Crystal Haven Hellgate. A muffled voice came from above, inaudible from the cargo hold, but I felt the plane descend. We would land shortly.

"Wake up, Emi." I nudged her quietly.

She raised her weary head from my lap and rubbed her eyes, "What is it?" she was still half asleep.

"We're almost there, we need to be ready to run when the plane lands, okay?"

"Okay, Yuri." she yawned as she stretched her arms.

We hid while the plane came to a stop and patiently waited for the cargo to be unloaded. There was an opening, and we made our way to the fence in search of the escape the elusive Chris had promised.

"Okay, sis…" I said, turning back to see her as she waved innocently toward the airport, "What are you doing!? Don't draw any attention, you'll get us killed! The SAS has eyes everywhere, and those people will turn on us just like the others."

How else could I tell my little sister how much danger we were in? I couldn't tell her the truth, I couldn't put that weight on her. The SAS was enacting a second witch hunt, only they'd skip straight to the bullet in the head.

She became sheepish, "I'm sorry, I know, but I was waving to the funny looking guy in the window." she said, and pointed toward a window that gave a view of the airport lobby.

I saw him, a man in a red, sleeveless, hooded jacket watched us. His blood red eyes were burned into my mind, and I felt only fear. Then, casually, his gaze shifted to Emi, and my heart skipped a beat as he raised his hand. I could almost feel my skin go pale and I expected the worst. His face shrouded, his expression blank, but he waved back and Emi giggled.

I pulled her through the torn fence, and she jerked her hand away, "Ow, what's wro…"

I interrupted her, "That's a Sleeper, we need to run now!" and her face froze with terror.

She didn't say another word, she understood the horror all too well, we both did. I took one final look back at Red-Eyes and security had surrounded him. As I nudged Emi to move forward, I could hear her teeth chattering, and tears ran from her dead eyes like when mom… No, I'd never let that happen again.

The last six months had been hell, "Mom would want us to be strong…" I told her as I fought against my own tears, "No matter what, I'll protect you." I said as I hugged her shivering body, "I swear…"

I was cut off by an incredible explosion from the airport that cast a hateful red light upon our backs. Emi broke free from my arms in a mad dash, and I chased after her. We ran for longer than I thought possible, but it still didn't seem far enough. We had escaped that Sleeper, but we were in a whole new world of trouble. For a soldier, facing the dangers was suicide, but it was the only option we had.

I held onto Emi as tight as I could, and she clung to me as she shook with fear. Everyone around us on the streets could be our next enemy. As we looked out, we saw the homeless littering the landscape. I saw a woman knelt on the sidewalk trying to feed a little girl leaning against a wall.

"Come on, honey." she said with a smile, "You need to eat to get your strength up." she said as she tried to spoon feed her something from a can that definitely didn't look like food, "There sweetie! Isn't it yummy?"

There was something wrong with that woman. Couldn't she tell the girl was dead? She was rotting away as bugs fed on her. I turned Emi away, it was too horrible. As I did, I saw two men in torn clothes fighting over a rat they were lucky enough to find and had been cooking over a flaming barrel.

I spotted a prostitute as she leaned against a building, and she looked at us. As we passed her, she rushed toward me.

"Sir, will you please buy something, anything?" she said as she tried to grab me, "I'll do whatever you want, just buy something from me, please!" she begged.

She got down on her hands and knees as she gripped my arms. Her face twisted in fear and sorrow, and tears ran down her face as she pleaded.

"Please, I have to feed my kids. If they don't eat soon, they're going to starve. You have to buy something from me, I beg you!"

I instinctively said, "I don't have any money." even if the fact I was a kid was far more important.

I broke away from her and she wailed, "I'll be gentle, I'll perform any service you want. I don't care. I won't judge you, I just need to feed my children."

"I'm sorry lady, we don't have any money. I couldn't even if I wanted to."

"Fine!" she screamed, "Be that way!" and her face twisted in rage as she flipped out, "If I ever see you again,

I'll cut your fucking dick off! You hear me, you bastard, I'll cut it clean off!?"

This was the world, it didn't care about itself, let alone kids. No one would bat an eye at a woman sleeping with a twelve-year-old boy. The government spent all their resources fighting Sleepers. It didn't have the free time to protect the people from each other. Then I caught a fine example of the "government" at work.

Two SAS soldiers were harassing a woman in the back of an alley. That's what happens when they'll take anyone they can get. The scum of the earth joined for power and authority. They hid behind a banner of justice to get what they wanted. Suddenly, the man lifted his gun and beat her over the face with the butt of it.

"Come on, are you a Sleeper?" he asked as he leaned in, "Because I see no reason why you would turn down a strong, upstanding soldier like myself."

I grabbed Emi and covered her mouth before the soldiers knew we were there. She fell to her knees as I felt her try to cry from behind my hand.

I peered around the corner and saw the woman's face bloodied, "Please, no, I've got a family..." she said as blood gushed from her mouth.

"Please?" he said as he feigned confusion, "I'm pretty sure I said please drop your pants and spread your pretty legs. I guess please doesn't mean what it used to anymore."

The woman with him put her hand on her hip slightly above her holstered weapon, "She has to be a

Sleeper. Why else would she refuse? She's afraid of being found out."

There had to be something I could do to save that woman, but she'd turn on me just as fast.

Then he let out a sick grin, "Yeah, that's what I was thinking, too! And there's only one thing to do with Sleepers."

"No, please! I'm begging you.." and I saw the light from her eyes fade as he put a bullet between them.

Her body fell lifeless as he passed his gun off to his partner, "Take this!" he smiled as he undid his pants, "I don't think she'll be saying no anymore."

"The next one is mine, and remember, dead men don't wiggle! So, don't get trigger happy!" she said as she lowered her pants and sat down with her hand between her legs, "I can at least enjoy watching this round. Now, put on a good show for me!" she moaned.

What was wrong with those sickos, had everyone lost their minds? I knew things were bad, but for Christ's sake, they just murdered that woman for sex! I thanked God I had pulled Emi away before she had seen any more nightmare fuel. I could see it in her eyes, the horrors of that night were coming back in her mind. There was no turning back for us, we had to fight onward.

If we didn't move, we would be next. I had been taking us toward the meet point with Chris, but it was still another couple of blocks. It may as well have been a million in that hell. Then I felt Emi go into a panic attack. I wanted to say that some part of me was still that same twelve-year-old who would have been scarred by what he had seen. Though, you learn to sleep at night once you've seen the nightmares long enough.

Emi was still so young, and I needed to protect my baby sister. I lifted her and ran as fast as I could. I ran until I found somewhere without people. For someone so innocent, she had seen so many horrible things. She remembered that night clearly, the night mom... I was a bastard of a son, I couldn't protect mom, and I couldn't even remember what happened.

I just woke up with everything covered in blood, and Emi as she stood there in shock. She stood with a dead look in her eyes as she shook like she was now. I laid her down and held her tightly as she gasped. She mumbled something about a man, a monster, and a demon, but I didn't understand. I didn't know what to do, the only time it had ever been worse than this, was that night.

I cried, I didn't know how to help her, I thought she was going to die. Without warning, I was hit on the back of the head, and I fell on my chest with a ringing in my ears. It took everything I had to look up to see a homeless man in tattered clothes, but his gun drew my undivided attention.

"What do we have here!?" he said with a grin full of missing teeth, "Two kids no one will miss!"

I tried to run for Emi, but he kicked me hard in the stomach. As I felt the air escape my lungs, he beat me across the face with his gun, then kicked me away. I tumbled back and smacked my face hard on the concrete.

"Don't make me tell you lived in oracle, you're picking at all!" he shouted incoherently as spit flew from his mouth.

He was spouting utter nonsense, and I could barely see anything. I spit up blood and felt one of my teeth slide out of my mouth. It scraped my lips and tapped against the ground. I saw Emi shaking as she extended her hand toward me. The look on her face tore me up inside.

She was more afraid for me than herself. I reached out to her, but he stomped on my wrist with all his weight. He raised his gun, not at me, but at Emi.

"You want to watch her die, because I do?" he grinned, "Ever see a man's brain splatter across the wall and his body fall limp? It's a beautiful thing!"

I felt my heart pound against my chest as I looked into her eyes. Her scared little eyes screamed out for me, she just wanted her worthless brother. In them, I saw flashes of that night, the look in our dead mother's eyes as I stood over her lifeless corpse. I saw the way things used to be, the way that both of them used to smile. Those were happier times that were ripped away from us, and I couldn't save our mother.

I saw my little sister's life about to fade away, and there was nothing I could do. I cried and screamed out as I saw his finger tighten on the trigger. All I was worried about was seeing my sister smile again. I was going to lose the most important thing to me. I looked into her eyes and as the tears rolled from them, my chest filled with pain.

All the love I felt for my innocent little sister turned to blinding rage. My heartbeat was deafening. Without knowing how, I found my teeth sinking into his ankle. The feeling of his hot blood as it poured into my mouth was sickening, but I bit until I tore out a chunk of flesh. He stumbled back and screamed as he tried to swipe his gun toward me.

Out of the corner of my eye, I saw a shard of metal and grabbed it on instinct. Before I knew it, he was on the ground as I plunged it into his face.

"I'll fucking kill you. You hear me, I'll fucking kill you!" he screamed until I could no longer hear any words.

By the time I realized what had happened, I was sitting on his chest with a searing hot pain in my hand. I dropped the metal shard and looked at my blood soaked hands in horror. I looked down at him, the man who had tried to kill us. He wasn't a man anymore, there was nothing left of his face that could be called that. It looked like a pile of raw hamburger that had been mashed into a paste.

Had I done that to him? I wanted to say I was shocked by what I was capable of, or that I was sorry I had taken his life. That's what the old me would have said, but my sister was alive. I grabbed his gun without hesitation and ran to Emi. She looked on in horror as she gazed upon my blood covered face.

All I could do was hold her as she cried. I had tried to protect her, but in the end, I had only hurt her more.

"I'm so sorry, Emi, I'll make this right. I don't know how, but I'll find a way!"

At that moment, a chill went down my spine, and I could feel something evil was out there. The street lights went out one by one, and I knew we had to run. Before I could do anything, I felt a touch on the back of my neck. A painful tingling sensation cascaded through my body as it locked up. The last thing I remembered seeing was my reflection in a puddle as I fell to the ground and blacked out.

I saw it, the blood-soaked face that had caused Emi to cry again. It was my face, the face of a monster…

…

… …

… … …

I remembered the warmth of my mother's hug as she put me to bed. She was the kindest woman I had ever known. She made me feel at peace, and I fell asleep quickly. All I remembered after that was waking up in the dead of night to my sister's scream. I could barely stand, and my vision was blurry.

The house was ablaze and smoke burned my eyes and lungs. There was no hesitation as I ran to the door and burned my hand on it. I heard my mother scream, and I felt no pain as my skin burned. I didn't think twice about myself as I ripped open my bedroom door. There was a sudden backdraft of flames that shot into my room.

I fell back, but got to my feet and jumped into the fire without a second thought. The hallway crawled with a fire that almost seemed alive. I didn't stand around to be afraid of the flames and darted down the hall. When I made it to the living room, I found Emi cowering in the corner. My mom was yelling as she barricaded the windows.

People were trying to break into the house. Everywhere I looked, they were attacking relentlessly. Only, these people weren't normal, they were destroying heavy wooden furniture with their bare hands. They had a vicious look on their face, and their eyes glowed red. Emi rocked back and forth on the floor and screamed as she held her head.

I didn't know what to do, and before I could move a muscle, they busted in. They ripped the door from its hinges, and one lifted a dresser over their head. Another smacked my mother and sent her flying across the room. She hit her head hard, and so much blood came out. I ran to her as fast as I could, as the horde charged at us.

As I blinked, the world changed around me. I was standing there drenched in blood and my clothes in tatters. The room had been splattered red, like buckets of paint were splashed against the walls. I looked down at my hands, and saw my mother between my fingers. She had chunks of her flesh missing all over.

The monsters that had attacked us lay strewn across the floor like jigsaw pieces. I fell to my knees and cried as I grabbed my mother. I shook her, again and again, but she wouldn't move as I called out to her. I couldn't understand why she wouldn't wake up, she had only been bitten a couple of times, nothing that could kill her. I looked back to Emi as if hoping she would know how to wake mom, but she stood still.

She looked forward with a dead gaze and remained motionless. I walked to her and tried to move her, but she only swayed as I nudged her. Her gown was soaked with tears as her eyes dripped like leaky faucets. Not knowing what to do, I reached out and held her. In my arms, she was shaking like a leaf, but my words would not calm her.

I gripped my eyes closed tightly as I tried to fight my own tears. As they slowly opened, I felt a sharp pain on my neck, and my face was wet. I looked around and saw the alleyway we had been in, and then it hit me. I remembered being attacked and panic sunk in. I looked for Emi, but I was alone.

Once I realized she was gone, I tried to run, but I couldn't stand. My neck hurt so much, and my body felt disorganized. As I stumbled into a wall, I saw a window. I looked into it to see the back of my neck. When I pulled my shirt collar back, it stung, and I soon saw why. There was a handprint on my neck, burned into my skin.

A Sleeper had attacked me and stole my sister. I was overwhelmed with sadness and rage. My brain couldn't decide whether to cry or twist my face in anger. All I could think of was the Sleeper from the airport. He had taken an interest in her and must have followed us.

How could I have been so stupid? How could I let her get taken? She was all I had left in this world, and I couldn't protect her, just like I couldn't protect mom. I ran to the streets hysterically, but could see her nowhere. Even if the SAS weren't hunting us, the ones we saw would kill me for looking at them. I was just a kid, what in God's name could I do!?

I didn't stand around. The cold air felt like needles filling my lungs as I ran, but I ignored the pain. For Emi, I would turn this city upside down ten times over.

I wandered the city in my search, and in no time I'd been walking for more than an hour. My legs were tired, and the only bench I saw was occupied. After being nearly molested and almost murdered, any risk seemed like suicide. It was getting really cold, I didn't have a jacket, and I was so hungry. I decided to sit but kept my hand on the gun in my pocket.

I sat opposite of him and kept quiet as I thought about my sister. It was hard not to cry when I thought of all the things he might have been doing to her. My mind jumped to the worst possible scenarios, and after several minutes, I'd had enough silence. There was a picture of her in my wallet, and I retrieved it with my free hand.

"Excuse me, have you seen my sister?" I asked.

He leaned in, but I couldn't see his face past his hood, "No..." he said with a grunt.

"Thanks..." and he motioned with his fingers in acknowledgment.

Sitting was only making me colder, so I put the picture away and stood. I didn't want to become an ice sculpture and couldn't waste any more time. As I left, I kept an eye on him, but he didn't move. What felt like minutes slipped away like seconds as the air got colder. The wind was worse, my body was numb.

The snow had distracted me long enough for a man to bump into me as he stepped out of a building. I nearly fell as he scared me shitless. He looked gigantic, like he could lift a horse with one hand behind his back. If that guy started anything, I was dead. It looked like bullets would bounce off the guy!

He looked at me, "Hey, kid!" he said solemnly, "You're gonna catch a cold dressed like that, ya know. Here, take this!" and he put his jacket around me, then left.

I was confused as to why he had done that. The kindest thing anyone had done for me in a long time was threatening to cut my dick off. At that point, I was freezing and the jacket was warm. It would keep me from dying from the cold, but my search for Emi was getting nowhere. There weren't any people left on the streets, but I had to keep going. Then the hunger came again, I hadn't eaten in days. My stomach felt like it was twisting.

I saw the man from the bench earlier, he was leaning against a streetlight. I hadn't seen him in over an hour, yet he had caught up. Was he following me? Just to be safe, I took the next street and walked away. Before long I saw him again.

Suddenly, he was at every turn. It was humanly impossible to move that fast, unless... he wasn't human. When the thought hit me, fear consumed my every fiber. He was a Sleeper. My feet were running before I knew it, and loud footsteps came from all around. At first, I thought he was following me, but something felt off.

I got a distinct feeling he wasn't after me and stopped. A thick, unnatural fog rolled in, but there were rules. There must have been another Sleeper, they were hunting in a pack. The fog was the perfect cover, and then, I heard the second set of footsteps. It was a tapping against the asphalt, high heels, maybe, and the shriek of a woman echoed between the buildings.

"Aaah! Don't kill me!" she cried.

Apartments lights went dead, they were afraid. I couldn't blame them, Sleepers were monsters. Hell, I felt safer to know it wasn't after me. Safety was around the corner, I just had to leave. Saving my own ass was easy. Turn around, and never look back.

"Don't hurt me!" she cried again, "Whatever I did, I'm sorry!"

It was pitiful, this woman had no defense against them, and she was outnumbered. How was a kid going to help, I'd be a paper wall covering a bank vault? If I did save her, she'd turn on me, or it could be a trap to lure in idiots. Her every scream turned my stomach. I just had to keep walking and live, it was that easy.

It's hard having a conscious in hell. I checked the gun before I ran toward her screams. As I stumbled in the fog, I followed the sounds of her heels. That was easier said than done, the echoes were confusing. Abruptly, her scream cut out preemptively, but I could tell exactly where she was. I heard sounds of a struggle, only worse.

She gargled just before her screams stopped altogether. I held the pistol tightly and moved slowly as I saw a single figure in the fog. It was feminine, so I moved closer.

I reached out and spoke softly, "Hey, lady, are you okay?"

She was standing alone, but wasn't moving. I touched her arm, and she toppled over. What I saw was enough to make someone vomit, and I would have if I had eaten in the past week. I doubled over, and nothing came up as I gagged. Every time I thought it was over, I gagged again, it was horrible. She was all but completely deformed, she looked like a nightmare, but still human on some level.

Her head was split down the middle like a Siamese twin, and her mouth was slit back with more teeth than I could count. She had more fingers on one hand, and a second forearm was coming from her elbow. There was a third leg coming out of her stomach, but it was worse than all of that. She was still "changing", a third, then a fourth slit opened on her head, and behind the first was an eye. The second stopped forming halfway, and never opened, then... she stopped breathing.

She had been alive during all of it, I could only imagine her pain. It was wrong of me to say, but she was dead, and I could get the hell out of there before it happened to me. As soon as I stopped gagging, I ran as fast as I could. On the way out, I bumped into the man who had been following me.

I fell and he said, "Wrong time, wrong place kid. You've seen me, now, I have to kill you. Nothing personal..." he almost looked sad about it.

He lunged at me as I whipped my pistol out and shot several rounds into him, and he fell down dead on top of me, or he should have. His body lay lifeless, briefly, before becoming glowing smoke and drifted into the fog. Afterward, one by one they stepped out, I was surrounded by multiples of him. I thought I was a goner, until a light shone on me, and the sound of an engine roared loudly. There was this tough, badass looking biker dude sitting on a motorcycle, watching us...

CHAPTER 2
HOT HEAD

CRIMSON FLAMES, THE 27TH -- The hot-headed biker sat back in a chair as the patrons of the strip club went on with their lives.

Boom, boom, boom, the club music was so loud I couldn't hear myself think, "So, have you gotten him to tell you what these people are doing with all of them?" he asked, but he was more focused on the strippers sliding against the poles.

He interrupted me with his hand as he sipped his drink, "Let me guess, it's need to know. That man and his secrets, he needs to let loose and live a little." then he cut me off again, "And I know what you're going to say. Just because I'm looking, doesn't mean I've forgotten her." he said as a stripper straddled him, then he looked at me, "Okay, this stays between the two of us, ya hear me?"

MICHAEL ANDERSON

"I can keep a secret, baby!" she said.

"Oh, you can!?" he smiled as he ran his hands over her.

I motioned her to get lost, "What's your problem, asshole!?"

"No, Mr. No Fun is right." and he helped her to her feet, "We've got business to discuss."

"Okay." she wiggled her ass, "Call me when you're done!" she walked away and flipped me off.

I swear, the guy was built like a brick house, and women couldn't keep their hands off him. It takes more than a bunch of muscle to make a man, those girls were stupid.

"Knock, knock!" he said as he tapped his knuckles against the visor of my motorcycle helmet, "You gonna take that thing off?" I shook my head, "Yeah, you're right, you don't want to scare them off with that ugly mug of yours." then he began nursing his drink.

I casually reached over and tipped his drink as I relaxed in my chair, and it spilled into his lap.

He brushed off what he could, "Yeah, real mature, and who's acting like the child now?" I shrugged, "Fine, be that way, but you don't write, you don't call. Then, you suddenly come to my place of work and want my help hunting down some bad guy. I see how it's going to be, you're just using me to do your work.

It's not like I'm made of magic, that my sixth sense is as powerful as I am handsome, and I'm going to pick this guy out of a crowd the moment I see him..." then he turned

38

DEVIL INSIDE – THE MAN WITH CRIMSON EYES VOL. 1

serious, "He's here, just walked in." he pointed, "By the entrance, in the hood, he's definitely a Sleeper, and from the look of him, he's definitely the guy you're looking for." I patted him on the head, "I'm not a dog."

I passed a stripper on stage who hit on me, "Hey, baby, how about some private time?" I flipped her off, "Yeah, fuck you too, buddy!"

It was hard to follow the guy in the grey hoodie, he stayed close to the crowds. He passed the bar near the center stage, and I lost him. Suddenly, he was across the room. Had he doubled back on me? As quickly as I had found him, he was gone again, then popped up somewhere else again.

Was he a teleporter, "Something's up with this guy." came across my earpiece, "There's more than one now, and not like more Sleepers. They have the same energy, so, I'm thinking he can make copies of himself, and... Oh, look out behind you." he said calmly.

No sooner did he say that, did I turn to get hit over the head with a baseball bat. My helmet took most of the force, but it still dropped me to my knees, and there was panic in the crowd. I was surrounded by six of them, and one had a woman as a hostage.

He had the woman's mouth covered with one hand and held his other next to her head as he moved in, "What the hell are you following me for!?" he yelled.

"Mr. Chatty is the original, he has the highest concentration of energy, go after him." Mr. Know It All told me.

"Hey, come join me at the grand opening of the Atomic Busts in Midnight City this weekend." an ad on TV said, I could hear it now that the music had stopped.

As I stood the Sleeper yelled, "Get the fuck down and answer my question!" as the one with the bat swung again.

I caught the bat with one hand and drove the same fist into the son-of-a-bitch's face. My punch sent him flying back into the stage, then he flipped over its edge, and he flew across the room. Still holding the bat, I broke it over my knee and threw the two halves behind me. They smashed into the two jumbo TVs, and they shattered as I smiled on the inside.

"Shit!" he yelled, " You're a Sleeper too!? Oh well, you played your hand too early. You know the rule right, we ain't got but one each? So, your super strength won't help you now. I'll just fight you at a distance. Let's burn this asshole!!!" he yelled as they showered me with Molotov cocktails.

Everything in a ten-foot area, including me, went up in flames. When he knew what I knew, his face was going to be priceless. The flames swirled up around me and only a frost remained.

"How the hell!? We only get one power!" he yelled, "It was you wasn't it!?" he shouted as he pointed to the dumbass who was still calmly sitting as he sipped his drink.

"Who me?" he pointed to himself, "Nah, ain't me. It's all that one." he was an ass.

"You're lying, Sleepers only get one!" I shrugged, and moved closer, making him panic, "Stay back or I'll kill her!" but I moved closer, "That's it!" then came a sick smile, "This is my favorite part!"

"No! Don't do it!" Mr. Hero begged as he jumped from his seat, "She has nothing to do with this, don't hurt her!"

He placed his hand on her, she violently shook, and what I saw happen next turned my stomach. She ripped and split open all over, and before I knew it, someone was coming out of her like they were trapped inside. He pushed her at me as he ran away, and she died in my arms as his copies surrounded me.

"That son-of-a-bitch!" I heard, " How dare he harm an innocent woman!" he crushed his glass with his bare hands, "You go after him. I'll handle these guys myself and catch up."

He was angry, he had been in a bad place since we met up, but there was a fire burning in him now. He could handle the shitheads, so I gently set the woman down and jumped over the copies. I nearly made it to the ceiling as I flew toward the front wall. I swept my foot out, and the wall exploded out onto the streets with one kick. When I landed, I saw the snow, but more importantly, he was gone.

The streets were quiet and cold, but the snow had yet to accumulate. He had gotten quite the lead on me, but I spotted him dart out of sight at the corner down the street. I wasn't jumping city blocks to catch up, so I hotwired a crotch rocket just outside the bar. It was something I had learned on the streets as a kid. Once the engine revved, I took off like a bat out of hell and followed him down the next street.

The snow wasn't that thick, but any snow presented its own problems for even the best drivers. Underneath the slush, the road and sidewalks stuck out like sore thumbs through the footprints left behind. I thought it would be smooth sailing, but I didn't have that kind of luck. The trail had overlapping prints, then I noticed they were made by the same shoes. He had made more copies.

His tracks split five ways, and it was impossible to track the real one. The murdering bastard thought he'd gotten away, but I'd find him. I was going to follow a trail and beat the first thing I found. It might not be the right one, but it would make me feel better. Soon, I caught up to one running through an open field.

I didn't hesitate to race in after him, and I leaped off the bike. I wasn't going fast, but it still hurt when I smacked into him. We tumbled to the ground, but I got up first. He rolled away, and I kicked up a spray of mud. He flung his hand out to grab me, but I evaded and sent him flying like a rag doll with a kick to the stomach.

I jumped above him about head high and dropped my foot into the ground. I punched him in the face, and he burst into a cloud of multicolored energy. I knew my fist could go through a man's head, but what the fuck was that shit!? The energy fled, and my instinct to chase gave in. Even with a motorcycle, I lost it after several blocks, and fuck, that pissed me off to no end.

I wanted to beat his face in so badly that I was about to add a new pothole to the pavement when a heavy fog rolled in and distracted me. He had always hunted behind the thick fog at night. If I didn't stop him quickly a woman was going to die. I headed into the fog, but I couldn't see more than a few feet ahead. I turned the bike off and coasted with my foot.

My wheels popped and crackled on the asphalt loudly. To keep it from echoing, I slowed down and heard a woman scream. I could hear her high heels, so she was running and an idiot. She needed to take them off so she could run rather than letting the psychopath know exactly where she was. Survival was more important than looking good.

I was tossed to the ground by a metal pipe to the head. I tumbled, and the bike slid down the street. When I got to my feet, I was surrounded by copies, I guessed I was on the right track. I was rushed and brushed one away before I put my fist through his chest. He exploded into the same multicolored energy that flew away.

There were three more, and two of them charged me like idiots. I could have crushed them, but I had an idea. I dropped under a punch and grabbed him by the leg. Using him, I swept the second off his feet and slammed the first into the ground. He exploded, and the light traced the same path.

I figured it was a safe bet the energy was returning to the Sleeper. When the one with a pipe came at me, I got another idea. I fended off their attacks and knocked their weapons away before I grabbed them by the necks. They tried to fight, but I endured their weak ass punches as I walked them to my bike. I used my foot to stand it up and sat down as the two tried to get away the moment their feet touched the ground.

The one in my left hand, well, I squeezed until his head popped off… and he exploded like the others. There wasn't a moment to waste, and I was right behind it. It was hard to maneuver with the little bitch as he kicked and screamed next to me. There was obviously going to be some difficulties, that's why I brought two. Not long after I lost it, I turned to the dead man in my right hand, paused for a moment, then popped him.

Luckily, he burst into energy, but I lost it several blocks later. That's when I heard gunshots, and I was feeling lucky. So, I followed them into a thicker fog. I turned on the bike's headlights and tried to navigate the fog. I came across two figures, a kid on the ground, and the other was him.

I sat there and shone the light on them for a while before they noticed.

"Who the fuck are you!?" the Sleeper shouted, but the boy seemed paralyzed.

I wasn't letting him get away again, I was ending it. So, I stepped out into the light.

"You!" he said, "What, you got a hard-on for me or something? Things will go differently without that Sleeper helping you."

Then his flesh twisted, and ripped, truly a disgusting sight. Copies walked out of him like an assembly line. Before I knew it, there were five in all. He was ready for a fight, and I motioned the kid to leave. He ran as I cracked my knuckles and my neck to get into the mood. I held my hands out and felt the energy in the air.

There wasn't much, but I needed to clear the fog. The energy slipped from the air as I tugged on it. The fog froze instantly as the moisture in the air chilled, and it formed ice crystals that fell to the ground as snow.

"How the hell!?" he screamed as he became completely visible, "How are you doing this!? No one has two powers!" he looked around, "You're cheating! He's here isn't he, he has to be!?"

It was me, it had been from the beginning. In this game, knowing is the difference between life and death, the first to figure out the other's power usually wins. You have to use your power as quickly and as creatively as you can. The more complicated the usage, the better. Sometimes you get lucky, and your power is so monstrous it can't be stopped.

It's something even I have to worry about, because no matter how powerful you are, we're all still human... except for him. I tried hard to forget him, but every now and again he slipped back in. I had to keep my head in the game, and nothing made me feel better than putting the beatdown on some punks. I had to fight carefully, one touch and he could do whatever that was to me. So far his copies didn't seem like they could, and I'd been stupid enough to give them the chance too.

"I'll fucking kill you if you get in my way!" he shouted.

They always threw out threats when they know they've lost, it was so funny it made me want to laugh. I was going to end it fast and pushed my palm into one. Contact was quick, after all, I didn't know his limits, and he flew back into the others. It was going to be tricky to fight because I couldn't see the real one, unlike a certain asshole I knew. I didn't want to accidentally kill him, my paycheck depended on it.

My strength had to be held back and I charged them with my fists at the ready. From between them, I deflected one punch and dodged another. They left themselves open, so, I put a punch to one's jaw and dug my other fist into the ribs of the second. The first fell from my love tap, bitch had a glass jaw, but the second one shrugged off the rib shot. It was weird, I should have broken a rib or two with my strength, maybe he was a copy.

I laid a volley of punches up his chest and planted a good one on his sternum. He took them all well enough to take a swing at me while I was playing him like a musical instrument. He was too slow, and I drove my palm up under his chin. He stumbled, I saw my chance to test him and lunged in with my pointer finger readied. I rammed it into his stomach and he popped.

This time, however, it ran into the fog that had begun filling back in and fizzled out. I threw my hands out and converted it into snow to find what I assumed was the real one. I was pretty damn sure of it, and was willing to bet on it! So, I reached under the back of my jacket and pulled out two magnums and began to shoot everyone but him. They became light, and return to him, but I need to make sure he was real.

I pistol whipped him unconscious, and there was blood on my gun. The copies never did bleed, I was confident he was the real bastard. Before I could do anything else I heard a noise and pointed my gun in that direction. A trash can had fallen over, was I wrong, was he another fake? I walked closer, but there was no one. That's when I heard footsteps behind me and turned, only to be hit again.

It hurt like a bitch and caused me to scream out, "FUCK! Right in the tit!"...

CHAPTER 3
THE GIRL WHO WORE RED

ELSEWHERE IN CLEARCREST, EARLIER THAT NIGHT -- The girl known only as Little Red was on the hunt once more.

The warehouse was dark and musty, it was damp and leaking everywhere from the rain. There was a bad smell, a rancid odor I couldn't place. It was rundown and falling apart, but the neighborhood was worse. I wanted to leave quickly, the place felt wrong. So, I lifted my skirt and slid out one of the vials strapped to my thighs.

I dusted off a place to sit and pressed my skirt to my legs to protect against the cold cement floor. With my legs crossed, I uncorked the vial and sprinkled the contents inside the chalk outline. A simple mixture of spices and herbs from your average kitchen. The candles provided light and incense cleared the air. A personal effect would have helped, but I wouldn't need one if I knew who she was.

The spell was going to take some time to reach her without one. For the magic to work, I needed sharp focus. It was going to be hard, like your boyfriend on prom night. The work had been done, and the stage had been set for better or worse. My mind drifted and focused on the girl, and I hoped retracing my steps would help.

A few days earlier, I was on the net as usual...

LOCATION UNKNOWN, THE 23RD...

[AnonymousUser416]: They're so springy and perky! ;) I love your long blonde hair and blue eyes.
[TheBig8====)]: Best girl on this site.
[Anon6969]: How can you justify that? She's the hottest girl on EARTH!
[IamNotRon...]: Look Ma, I'm on page 49!
[LittleRed]: Hey guys! Thanks for coming.
[TheBig8====)]: No, thank YOU!
[IamNotRon]: Ahhhh, I saw what you did there!
[InfiniteSplit]: How you doing, Red?
[Shadow]: Hey, Red, good to see ya.
[LittleRed]: Hey, Infinite and Shadow. You guys doing good?
[InfiniteSplit]: Almost mugged, so not bad.
[Shadow]: Just getting by.
[ThatGuy69]: I usually prefer a carpet to go with my drapes. But silky smooth is good too.

[LittleRed]: Oh, no, are you okay, Infinite?

[InfiniteSplit]: Yeah, there were a couple SAS soldiers nearby. The only damn time they've been useful. I bolted before they could shake me down themselves.

[Shadow]: I told you, you need to get a gun, a really big one like me. Nobody will fuck with you then.

[InfiniteSplit]: Too expensive, besides, I don't like guns. I'd probably just arm the thug anyway.

[TheDuke]: Where's your cat?

[ThatGuy69]: It's between her legs, moron!

[LittleRed]: No fighting, enjoy the boobs;) Bastion, he's catching rats or something. Glad you're okay, Infinite.

[InfiniteSplit]: Oh my god… Did anyone else hear!? There's been another attack, and they're saying this one isn't the Jack the Ripper knockoff. This woman was ripped to pieces, they said it looked like an animal ate half of her. So, great, we've got another psychotic killer running loose, and this one eats people. What is the SAS going to do about these Sleepers!?

[LittleRed]: Guys, I've got to go! Something's come up. I'll treat you to something special next time….

The cam show went dark, and I called an old acquaintance using my computer.

She answered quickly, "Girl, calm down! I know what you're gonna say, I just found out myself." she was Louis Samba, a voodoo practitioner, someone I'd known for a long time, "I was about to call when you… Girl, why you naked!? Put that away before you invite the devil in!"

"Why I'm naked is not important." I said as I dodged her question, "It has to be her, right?"

"Baby…" she shook her head, "There's a cluster of things that go bump in the night that could have done this. I know you have to check it out like the others. I'm only worried you're getting your hopes up. Don't go looking for devils, unless you're ready to find them, Sug."

"Yes, but get me everything you can." I pleaded. "You know I will, just take it easy. Are you sleeping well?"

"Yes…" I said, looking away.

"Now, I know that look." and she did, "If the dreams…"

"I have to go!" the call disconnected, "Damn, gotta rub one out to calm down!"

…

The next few days were spent hunting for clues as I sifted through Louis's information. Through the years, I'd tracked down many strange occurrences, investigating gruesome murders became a dark hobby. I was compelled, it was an urge to seek the elusive figure from my past. Looking for a ghost makes a person question their sanity, left wondering if anything is real. Something that creates an obsession that preys on you, stirs your inner demons.

The trail would go cold before it was ever hot, then seemingly pick up elsewhere. A killer that had claimed hundreds of victims and hundreds more newspaper articles. Thousands of images and tales, my fingers were stained black from the ink. Walls lined with news clippings, the images of victims haunted my sleep. I lived and breathed for the chase and through obsession, my mind was a shrine to their work.

With the world's end, my sanity clawed me inside and out. The Revelation Outbreak turned the world upside down, people lived in fear. Thousands of new monsters to haunt the night, and the government, a drug to keep the people afraid. All information on the murder was covered up, palms were greased, and people were kept quiet. The powers that be hid the truth, the reality of fighting a war already lost.

There was nothing to gather from vague second-hand accounts of half-truths. So, I packed anything that might help me, books, articles, etc., and prepared my luggage. With each passing day, things slipped from me, things I didn't notice fade. I collected clothes for the days, maybe weeks I'd be gone. My meticulous notes were the only thing that kept my thoughts from bleeding together as I began my journey to Clearcrest.

CHAPTER 4
RUMBLE IN THE SHEETS

"The pulsing beats, blasting music, flashing lights, and angels sliding steel. Sitting back with a smile, I sip my amber elixir like a king. Angels floating on air, spinning round and round. They shoot me glances and lick their lips. They sway to the music as they dance under the light.

Shedding their clothes on hand and knee with long locks flowing over silk skin. Baring it all, swaying closer as our bodies met. Grinding, twisting, and pumping up and down. Love, lust, and flesh pairing as one, reason lost to the sound of music. Minutes become hours in a world of carnal sin."

CRIMSON FLAMES, THE 27TH – EARLIER THAT NIGHT -- The Black Dragon enjoyed his night of fun. His chiseled muscles and strong jaw assured this every time.

After a long night of hitting the bar, downing the shots, and playing under the sheets, I still awoke from a good night's sleep. Yeah, sleep, that's definitely what you call it, and I was loving every minute of it. I could still hear the music from downstairs, and I could feel the beats through the floor. I had to wet my whistle, a guy needs his fluids. I reached to the nightstand for my beer and there was enough left.

I tossed the now empty bottle into the trash can, a perfect shot. Something stirred under the sheets. I lit the dark room with the table lamp and light rolled over the curves shaping the sheets. Hands caressed my stomach up to my chest, and I pulled the sheets back. I met a pair of blue eyes and the warmth of the soft skinned beauty pushing against me.

"Hey there, gorgeous!" I smiled.

"Hey there, you're not so bad yourself!" Fresca's lips were luscious.

The second set of hands pulled the sheets farther, "Last night was good, sexy." Sasha grinned.

"I aim to please, but you girls don't have to work me so hard. I didn't mean to wake you, but if you ladies will excuse me, I need to get to work."

"Oh, but we want to have more fun." there was unanimous disappointment.

"There's always time for fun later, but a man has a responsibility to reap the sweat of his brow." I said as I stood.

"And what a man!" Fresca said as she smacked my ass, and Sasha said, "That ass is so tight!"

"Ladies..." I sighed, "If you keep this up, I'll never get to work. As a man, I am honor bound, but at this rate, I'll never make it out of this room."

"Promise?" they grinned.

I slipped on my pants and fastened my belt, "Cute... But you girls need to get up too." and I slid open the curtains.

"Oww, that's bright!" Fresca said as she covered her eyes.

"Light is bad for hangovers, buddy." Sasha said as she buried her face in the pillows.

"Wouldn't know!" I smirked, "Besides, it's not even that bright. It's mostly cloudy, just like that last six months."

I grabbed my red satin shirt off a stack of magazines, they were actually rag mags. Not mine, honest, the room had been used for storage. I had gotten it all nice and neat, but last night got wild. I slid on my shirt and buttoned it up as the fourth member of our late night party stirred. She sat up holding her head in pain, she had drank the most.

Trish asked, "What time is it?" with a groggy tone.

I said, "It's a little after five-thirty." without giving it any thought.

Fresca dug her phone out of the nightstand, "It's five thirty-four... How do you always do that!?"

"A good internal clock, I guess." I was still focused on buttoning my shirt.

Trish asked, "How are you not hungover right now!? You drank so much... Ouch."

"How does it feel to never get a hangover, big guy?" Sasha asked.

"Since I've never been hungover, I can't compare." then I grabbed my suit coat.

It was a dark blue coat with white pinstripes running down it like my pants.

"Perfect inside and out, you must be built like a rock through and through." Fresca said.

"I have my flaws, but I did get dealt a good hand by the gods." I said as I popped my collar.

"I'll say you did." Sasha winked at me.

Trish yawned, "I'm going back to sleep, wake me up before our shift starts." and she crawled back under the sheets.

I walked from the window and headed to the door as I grabbed my fedora from the hat rack as I passed. The sound of music and the smell of booze hit me, I loved it.

I turned to the ladies, "I bid you farewell, ladies, but I must take my leave!" I took a bow and gave a smile.

"Bye, handsome!" Sasha waved with her fingers.

"See you later, sexy!" Fresca blew me a kiss.

I ducked to avoid hitting the doorway and closed the door as I said, "Bye."

I walked down the long staircase and kept my head slanted so I wouldn't bump the ceiling. The walls were a tight fit for me, but I couldn't beat the location and rent. I came out into a back room of the club, and I quickly made my way to the bar. Everything was already in full swing, the girls danced, and the guys were glued to the stage. Of course, the other side was for the ladies, and I remembered the time I danced for them.

I checked in with my boss at the bar, "Hey, man!"

"Vincent!" he smiled, "You heading out for a while?"

"No." I told him, "My shift is about to start, I'm going to clock in."

"You're always early, why not take it easy for once?" he chuckled, "Especially, after last night."

"A man's life is meant to be hard, otherwise he'll become lazy." I said and walked away.

"I really don't see what's so great about him." a guy at the bar said, "Sure, he's big, but..."

"Oh, will you be quiet, and drink this!" the boss said as he slammed a drink down, "He's on the clock now, you can take it easy."

It was the other bouncer, he was the only one before I came to town. I often got the sense he didn't like me, couldn't figure out why.

"Dude, sit back and enjoy!" I snapped my fingers and pointed at him, "There's plenty of work for everyone."

He flipped me off, to each their own, but hopefully, I'd be out of his way soon. I took my post, which eventually turned into partying on the floor with the guys, and the girls were all over me. Hours went by like minutes, but partying had lost its luster for me. I had no luck since I arrived in Clearcrest, and it was eating me up inside. After countless hours of searching, I had nothing for my trouble.

"Hey, Vincy!" a girl in angelic lingerie said, "How are you doing, honey?" I recognized Beth's voice, "What's wrong, you look down? Still can't find him?"

"No..." I softly said as I nursed my drink like a wounded animal in my chair.

"Are you sure he's still in the city. Could he have moved on?" she said with a caring tone.

"Yeah, I'm sure. I can feel him, he's in this city, but that's all I know." she sat on the arm of the chair as I spoke.

"Poor, baby!" and she pressed my head into her chest, "You have a good heart. Don't give up, you'll find him." then she looked me in the eyes, "But that's not what you're really upset about." I tried to avert eye contact, but she forced me to look at her, "What's wrong?"

I was hesitant, but finally told her, "It's this girl..."

"Honey, it's always a girl!" she shook her head.

"My girlfriend, she's in a bad way right now, and I had to leave her behind. I wanted to bring her with me, but let's say she isn't in any condition to travel. It hurt me bad, and the pain won't stop."

"I'm sure she understands, I'm sure she wants you to find him just as much as you."

I rolled my eyes, "No, she really hates him. It's a common consensus where I'm from." I said with a cringe.

I noticed she seemed a bit distracted, "Vincey, you've got a visitor."

I leaned my head back over the chair and saw someone clad in leather from head to toe with a closed off motorcycle helmet. They pointed at me and used their finger to motion me their way.

"A friend of yours?" Beth asked.

"Yeaaaaah… Something like that. I've gotta take care of this."

"Okay." and she stood and kissed me on the forehead before she walked away.

I wasn't thrilled about that one arriving, they brought almost as much trouble as he did. I followed the troublemaker down the hallway out back, it was unnervingly silent.

I had to break the silence, "Ya know, you can take the helmet off, right?"

"The helmet stays on!" you could feel the hostility.

"Whatever you want." I wasn't going to push the subject, not if I wanted my body in as few pieces as possible, "So, what brings you to my little piece of paradise."

"Outside. You wouldn't want the lowlifes to hear us and run away." and we opened the doors to the rear parking lot.

I saw a car parked out back, it sure surprised me a bit, "You have a working car, a military engine I'm guessing." I pulled my coat tighter in the cold air.

"I've got my connections." and my attention was drawn to the trunk.

Yeah, connections, also called, "Chris!" I thought, "Anyway…" I said aloud, "Why are you bringing me out here to freeze my butt off?"

"Cold!? Hadn't noticed."

"Yeah, you wouldn't. Just get on with it."

"I've got work in town, and I'm looking for a Sleeper. I believe he's called the Ripper, because he only target's women. I've been tracking him for a while."

"And you're intel would be?" then the trunk popped open, and there was a man bound, gagged, and bleeding all over, "There is a man... in your trunk."

"Meet my intel."

I flashed a fake smile, "Naturally, is there any other kind." I leaned in for a better look, he was breathing but beaten badly, "And you got this information, how?" and I heard cracking knuckles, "Of course you did." I sighed, "Ever thought of asking nicely?".

"Yeah…" and she slammed the trunk shut, "Left a bitter taste. Didn't care for it much."

"And was it necessary to beat him?"

"No, but it was fun." a casual answer, completely honest, and I expected nothing less.

"Okay, here's a question that's not stupid." I gestured for a moment with my hand, "This has what to do with me?"

"Well…" then came the nonchalant shrug, "I thought you'd like to know the local homicidal maniac likes to hang out here, in your club. Probably uses it as a hunting ground to pick his targets."

I smacked my face and slid my hand down slowly, "No, you wanted my help finding him. Your proficiency lies with punching stuff dead."

"Can't argue that, I do punch things really well." that was almost boasting.

"Fine… I'll help. I don't want anyone else hurt, okay?"

I was handed a small earbud, "How did you get one of these…" but I cut myself off, "Connections!" I faked enthusiasm, "Let's just get back inside… I have a feeling it's going to be a long night…"

CHAPTER 5
EGO DOES A BODY GOOD

TWO WEEKS EARLIER, THE 12TH -- The Gobbler rests comfortably in his twelve-bedroom mansion.

The night's moon shone its bright gaze, coating a light across the lands, artificially, of course. As I stared through my skylight, I imagined my white mansion atop the highest hill. Nestled firmly in the bosom of the acres of grasslands I owned, a modest addition to my collection. Nothing helped me feel more at home than to lay in bed with the sensation of white satin sheets against my skin. I was being gently lulled to sleep by the sounds of grasshoppers, but I was rudely stirred by a ringing phone. I reached into the dark and fumbled with it.

With a firm grip achieved, I lifted the phone from the receiver and articulately spoke, "Huh."

A familiar voice antagonized me, "Hello, traitor."

"Eric..." I said with a groggy tone, "I told you, you're level 10 cleric couldn't provide the same services the level 36DD barmaid could. It was an obvious choice for my level 20 sorcerer, she had very large jugs... and her boobs were nice too." and I slammed the phone down.

The phone rang again, "Damn it, Eric, I'm trying to sleep!"

"For the crime of Treason, you have been sentenced to death."

"Wait, you're not Eric, who is this!?"

"The man who's going to put the bullet between your eyes, Inferious!"

"Benson!" I grit my teeth, "Bastard, how dare you get your jollies harassing me while I sleep!"

"This is official business, Fatboy!" he boasted, "The Collective have found you guilty of treason, and by the 14, I have been sent as your executioner."

"I'm only going to say this once..." and I took a deep breath, "I'm the best there's ever been, I ran the FBI better than any agent before me. You've been gunning for me for years, and if you plan to carry out your little coup d'etat with some absurd setup to cover your ass with the 14... You better have an army to take this king off his throne!"

"Have a look!" he said as my computer monitor turned on.

I had to sit up in bed to see it. Once my eyes adjusted to the light, I saw Benson standing at my door with his ever so confident smug smile.

He held a paper up to the camera, "These papers come straight from their desks. How I wish I had some involvement in this, traitor!"

My eyes widened as I saw the Collective's seal upon the documents. I stood as I dropped the phone, and in a moment of weakness, I let out the shrill scream of a little girl. I ran to my computer and fiddled with my keyboard as I opened a second window. As I cycled the feeds, I saw soldiers everywhere like knights storming a castle, there WAS an army, maybe TWO! They had me surrounded, but they hadn't breached my defenses, I still had time. I ran through my room in my red boxers with white hearts and collected clothing and my emergency bag.

I quickly dressed as I picked up the phone, "Oh, shit! This is obviously a misunderstanding, if I could talk to them, I could explain myself... somehow."

"The Collective has no interest in your excuses." he smiled, "You sold our secrets to the highest bidder, and now, your so-called reign comes to an end!"

"Oh, come on!" I shouted, "If I decided to betray the Collective, they'd never have found out! Please, I'm too good!"

"Goodbye, Inferious!" the phone went dead as they cut the power.

"Please!" I said smugly, "Like I wasn't prepared for this. I have enough fuel and generators to let me download porn and fan-fiction for the rest of my glorious life. Nothing keeps me from my mistress, the Internet, not even something as silly as no electricity. You hear me?"

The generators kicked in and power returned to my systems seamlessly, and I began accessing my security. I put my fortress on lockdown and steel plates slid over every entrance. My firewalls were being taken down like shōji, and everything was undone as soon as I did it. They must have had a van full of nerds working against me. I chuckled, they'd need more than that to stop me, I hadn't had a challenge in a long time.

I heard helicopters fly in, and soldiers breached multiple access points on the first floor. That was fine by me, I just needed to buy time, and my security would do that. Throughout my mansion, traps were triggered, my favorite was the trick stairs that flattened out into a ramp that oozed oil. As I fought the digital intruders, I backed up my most recent files. Once that was finished, I was done, but they stormed my room from every point.

They had me dead to rights, or they wish they did, but I played them and was long gone. The thought of Benson's face when he realized he'd been duped would keep me warm for the nights to come. I was sure he was watching me, so I looped the video feed while I escaped and wirelessly fought back. I left him a present, and by the time he noticed my magnificent face on my computer screen, it was too late. The last thing he would hear was my laughter as my computer virus dug into my systems and overloaded everything, then boom...

A week later, I found myself in Fairwater, a city I thought I had escaped. It was a backwater place located in what was once West Virginia. I was held up in a hotel, it was run down, filthy, and the revolting smell of urine polluted the air. It certainly wasn't a place befitting of a man of my stature, but it was as off the grid as I could find on such short notice. With a little bit of bribery, I was able to get myself into room 213, even if the wallpaper was cracked and peeled.

It wasn't perfect, but they had a mini fridge I could use to stock goodies, woohoo. On the less damaged sections of the walls, I had hung every bit of useful info I had collected in my search for the truth. I had been nearly overwhelmed and found myself lost in thought as I looked out the window behind my desk. The sky roared with thunder as the rain poured atop the city streets. The multicolored neon lights made the rain droplets glow.

I was lost in the moment, oblivious to the mountains of documents piled up...

CHAPTER 6
WILL OF THE MEEK

LOCKHEART HOSPITAL, FAIRWATER, THE 27TH -- The Angel of Silence found herself looking Death in the eyes once again.

My hands were shaking badly, I couldn't stand the sight of all the blood. He was laying on the gurney dying, and I was supposed to save him. I'd never been able to control the shaking. Over the years, I had learned to hide it, they said you get over it by the first year, but... That made me feel even greener, as I was going on three years.

The man dying before me was more important than any of that. Stabbed, beaten, shot, and blood gushed from his motionless body. My mind bogged down with all the ways I could imagine him dying. I had to fight the fear that consumed me as it took root in my hands. I breathed in and out and focused on the classical music that came from my earphones.

I read the nurse's lips, "Are you sure?" he asked, "There's a low chance of saving him. I know it's wrong, but our time and supplies should be spent on people we can save."

Disappointed wasn't strong enough for how I felt. I wouldn't be able to live with myself if I didn't try. I snatched the scalpel from his hand and got started. I sliced into the wounds, but the damage was bad. There was internal hemorrhaging and his blood pressure was bombing.

They were hesitant when I pointed to the blood packs and gestured the type. Blood was valuable, so few people gave anymore, and the last donation was a week ago. I pointed again and they reluctantly hooked it up to the patient. His blood pressure increased, but it was still dropping. No matter how many nicks and gashes I sutured, the blood kept coming.

A knife wound had sliced his femoral artery. I used a hemostat, but it was no good. For every path I blocked, there were two more waiting. It was difficult to remove the deep bullets as the blood pooled up. He'd slip away if I didn't hurry. I was sweating as fast as he was bleeding, and it stung my eyes.

I removed one bullet after another, but there were too many GSWs. His blood pressure was dangerously low again, and I motioned for another blood pack. They refused, and I wanted to yell at them even if it wouldn't do any good. Time wasn't on my side, and the next bullet was lodged near the bone.

"I can save him!" I screamed in my head.

They grabbed me and one of their hands snagged my earbuds. I could hear the death siren of the heart monitor, he was dead. My tools were snatched from my hands and they pulled me away. I had to watch the man die. Through all the kicking, punching, and throwing, I was powerless as they dragged me out.

A part of me died with him as they took me to the Chief of Medicine's office... again. As a doctor, you have to try to save everyone, but they let some die to save the many.

"How many times do we have to have this conversation!?" he shouted, "You can't save everyone. Why must you insist on acting like a child when you fail. Most become somewhat desensitized by the loss within a year, but you still act as emotional as the day you started. Caring isn't a bad thing, but what you spend saving one could save ten.

I'm sad to do this again, but go home and get some rest." I couldn't help but cry, "Before you start, even if I wasn't allowed to kick you out, who would stop me? The rules of the old world died, we don't even have basic human rights anymore. We don't get paid, so technically we're all volunteers. It's not the end of the world, that already happened.

All I am doing is making sure you get some sleep, you've been here for nearly a week straight. The staff says you can't keep your hands steady anymore, and that could kill someone."

He sent me on my way, I was like a zombie going through the motions and eventually found myself in the locker room sitting under the shower. I often went there without knowing why. The hot water calmed me but left my clothes drenched. I'd sit there for hours sometimes, then stagger out, and change my clothes. This time was no different, and I walked out in a daze as I held my satchel tightly.

The air had been chilly for the past year, and my hair felt like ice. I had the hood of my coat pulled up to warm me. If I didn't keep my hands busy with something I was bound to sleep, so I needed some herbs. There was a local bar, the Squeaky Chair that managed to make alcohol from a common herb. I sometimes bought the unused parts and combined them with some of my own to help me sleep.

I shivered the whole way there, but it'd be warm inside. The back way was faster, but I soon wished I had taken the front door. The back of the bar was occupied by a group of bikers. I counted four, all were men and I tightened my grip on my satchel. My body naturally tried to take up less space, and I pulled my arms and legs closer. Somehow, I thought it would make me less noticeable. A sick feeling came over me, but they ignored me. As long as they left me alone, I wouldn't get scared.

I was nearly to the backdoor when I heard, "Hey there, pretty girl!" a fifth one said as he snuck up on me, "I think you're lost." and I completely lost my nerve.

I spun around on a dime, like a duck in a festival shooting gallery. My heart sank to my gut when I saw the others had surrounded me. It was a trap, and I'd fallen for it. My every exit had been covered. The wolves backed me against the wall.

The biker gang's leader stepped forward, "Sorry, the boss is in the middle of a little game, he doesn't like losing. We're guarding the exits in case someone tries to run." he smiled as he leaned.

I pulled away, but I could feel his breath against my neck. I clenched down harder on my satchel, it was my security blanket.

"The backdoor is off limits. Not that, every backdoor is off limits if you know what I mean…" he grinned, "Whoa, you're really pretty, you know that!?" he said as he lifted my head by my chin, "What are you, Japanese or Chinese? You've got that pretty little half-Asian thing going on here, and you sure can rock it!"

I began to shake, I was losing control. If he picked up on it, he'd pounce. If I lost it, all of them would die.

He looked me up and down, "I've got to ask, what's with the shorts if you're just going to cover up your pretty legs with these bandages?" he said as he pulled on one loop and snapped it against my leg.

I felt him touch my skin, and I jerked away. I'd shown weakness, and he'd exploit it. I prayed for the sake of their souls that they'd leave.

"Oh, you like that, don't you!" I could feel him fondling me with his eyes, "You have nice little breasts on you. I like 'em big, but if I play with them enough, maybe..."

I could feel the veil tearing, and they'd soon die.

"For the love of God!" the man yelled, "What in God's name is so damned important about that bag!? You've been clinging to it this entire time. Are you trying to say it's more important than me!?" he ripped it from me, "Let's see what you've got!"

I fell to my knees, it was going to happen again, the veil had torn. I grabbed my head and rocked back and forth in fear.

"The hell kind of freak do we got here, boys!?" he mocked me, "The bitch is carrying around a bag of hair. Wait..." he paused, "It's dyed blue... it's yours. The weird bitch is carrying around a bag of her own hair!"

As they laughed, my stomach knotted up. One of them had found the tear in the veil and was coming through.

"Wait..." he sounded confused, "There's something else, feels like glass."

I tried to warn him, but it was too late. When the veil tore, the surrounding area's pressure increased. When it came through, the pressure destabilized. It was like opening the hatch of a plane in mid-flight. I felt my ears pop as the air rushed through the tear and sucked my vial from his hand.

It shattered against the brick wall and exploded and sent needles in all directions. Every one of them was hit and fell to the ground motionless. No God, no, please don't punish me. God wouldn't punish me for it right, they did it to themselves. No, I'd be punished because I made a weapon!

They were only paralyzed, but I'd be punished for sure. I snatched my satchel and ran inside before I could make things worse. The veil closed behind me as I entered. They'd be safe from the beast on the other side.

The bar was packed with those that had lost faith and drowned their worries in alcohol. I wanted to tell them that God had not abandoned them but my voice would never reach them. With a deep breath, I stepped forward and bumped into someone.

The blonde man reeked of alcohol. With some fancy footwork, he spun around me. As drunk as he was, there was no way he should have had that much coordination. Then, I realized it was him, but he didn't seem to recognize me.

Instead, he took his hat off and placed it in my hands, "Hey, sir, old onto me at, would ya?" and he walked to the jukebox.

It's not proper for a child of God to look upon another with such disdain, but he was impossible. I moved on because his blasphemy seemed contagious to those around him. The barkeep spotted me and nodded before he slipped into the back.

I awaited his return at the bar but was tapped on the shoulder by another, "Hey, is that my hat!?" he asked.

I inched away from him until I was at the edge of my seat. I was frozen and no words would come to me.

"It is!" he smiled, "Where did you find it? Nevermind! You did good, lass…" he said as he pat me on my head, "Have a drink on me!"

He seemed to forget me immediately as a scene drew our attention. The blasphemer had somehow tripped and fell out the backdoor but managed to catch himself on the doorknob. He was sure to see everyone out back and would know it was me. Everyone in the bar drew their guns on him in the blink of an eye. There were times this man seemed like a genius, either truly smart or so stupid he was brilliant.

"Now, that's not something you see every day!" he said, "Why are five grown men laid out flat like porcupines in an alley when they could be in here getting laid out by the hard stuff!?" I sighed.

He was just a complete idiot! He came back inside, and people put away their guns. Soon, the bartender returned with the herbs, and we exchanged. He would have thrown them out anyway, so he gave me a good deal. Before I could leave, I heard a loud crash.

The blasphemer had strapped a helmet to his head and threw himself into a table. The bar was already on pins and needles, but he loved to poke the hornet's nest. I escaped in the chaos and ran for home. After a mile, I stood before the steps of my apartment building as I tried to catch my breath. Once in my apartment, I headed to the bathroom.

I took a shower to warm up and went to my kitchen. I grabbed my mortar and pestle, gathered the herbs, and put a kettle of water on the stove. As I was putting the herbs into the mortar to grind, I realized how low I was on the main ingredient! I began to cry, because without it, the mixture wouldn't work!

I'd have to spread it out and make it last longer. I prepared some hot tea with the water. I sat in my chair by the window, and sipped the tea as I looked out onto the city and took it all in. A grey sky may be bland, but it was calming in an otherwise chaotic world. When the tea was gone, I was off to bed. I hoped it would be a silent sleep…

CHAPTER 7
NINJA WITHOUT A CAUSE

ON THE OUTSKIRTS OF FAIRWATER, THE NIGHT BEFORE, AUGUST 26TH -- The White Tiger got in a light workout before bedtime.

"Nine hundred ninety-eight." I said as I brought my chest to my knees and back down again, "Nine hundred ninety-nine." I barely felt my stomach break a sweat as it was, "One thousand!" and I dismounted my legs from the tree branch.

I landed firmly on my feet as I always did and looked at the sky. I could almost see the moon behind the sea of clouds. It had better been a hallucination.

"Things always crushing my dreams!" I huffed.

Didn't matter, the day was over, and I didn't feel like I'd done any training. Peace was the worst motivator for training I had ever seen, I was getting lazy.

"Peace is so damn boring. What the hell am I supposed to do with peace? Don't make me knit, because I'm horrible at it. It makes grannies cry." I said as I shook my fist at the sky, "You know who you are!"

I hadn't broken a sweat, so I put my shirt back on, and skipped my bath for the night. I hoisted my belt, sword, and dagger that were resting against a rock and put them over my shoulder. My encampment wasn't far, and I traveled back in minutes. The fire was flickering out, right on time as it should have. I flicked my fingers as the wind blew it out.

I crawled into my tent, and I placed my sword on my right, within arm's reach. My pillow was soft as I put my head against it, and I pulled my blanket over myself. There wasn't a second that passed before I was dead asleep. I had dreams of walking out of exploding buildings, fighting hordes of enemies with a toothpick, and getting all the women. I awoke with faint sunlight on my face and exited my tent.

"My amazing dream was going so well until it became a nightmare with all those women." I cringed.

It was foggy, and the overcast sky only let light trickle through. From the hill I'd set camp on, I could barely see the river at the base. Dawn had recently broken, and I ran my fingers through my hair as I took in a deep breath of fresh air. The wind had carried a bad odor for almost a year and today was no different. Too much time had already been wasted, so I retrieved my belt.

I swiped my hand over the top of the tent, and with a soft click, it collapsed as I fastened my blades to my right hip. As I rested my wrist on my sword hilt, I picked up the pen my tent was in. After I put earphones in, I started my music, and slid my pen into my coat as I headed for the river. The solitude of camping on the outskirts of town made training easier but that meant a longer walk. A chill that could wake the dead was in the air and it sent a shiver down my spine as I reached the river.

I looked around to see if there were any dead, "Darn." I was disappointed there wasn't, "One day I will fulfill that dream of killing someone a second time."

I squatted for a moment, looked at my reflection, and used my hand to move my head. Sure enough, I was still as dead sexy as the day I was born, as if there was any doubt. I tapped my sneakers against a nearby rock to make sure they fit just right, and walked out onto the water. The ethereal energy that radiated from my feet reflected off the shallow areas of the water. Once across the river, I changed course to the main road, it was a lonely one to walk in the morning.

Not a soul was out, but in the distance, I could see the city welcome sign. As I drew closer, I could make out the details, not that it would say anything different from the day before. It was littered with graffiti, the usual juvenile antics of a child, a few of mine were up there too! When I stepped before the sign, I stared for a moment.

"Welcome to Fairwater! A quiet and happy city sitting safely and peacefully. Come join our happy community and start living life!" it read.

I tilted my head to the side as anything else with a neck could. I saw a barren wasteland of fire and brimstone outside the Hellgate that protected the city.

I looked at the sign and said, "I still say that's false advertisement." then left a moment later.

I continued on my way and shortly saw the first remnants of the city ahead. I approached a stone walkway with benches spaced evenly along the sides. It led to a large, circular area with a sizable fountain in the center. Without a thought, I flipped a coin into the fountain and continued on my way. My mouth felt parched, so I headed to a small bar nearby, the Squeaky Chair.

Outside was a large bouncer fellow, and I politely waved as I entered. I was hit with the thick aroma of cheap alcohol that was quite unpleasant. The bar was packed as one would imagine a post-apocalyptic bar would be, but everyone was crowded in the back. They were watching two men in a drinking competition. One, a biker with solid muscle; the second, a man of medium build in a silver trench coat and cowboy hat which did not make him as awesome as he thought he was.

Of course, I recognized the second and I didn't want to catch his crazy. I went to the table the farthest away and took a seat. While I waited for the hostess, I retrieved the book I was currently reading titled Anger & Management.

A moment passed and the waitress approached, "What would you like, sir?" she said with an unenthusiastic tone.

I said, "Water." so quickly I almost cut her off.

She wasn't happy about that and walked off with an attitude. A drunk man passed her as he staggered toward the front door. Unfortunately, he drew interest and walked over as he eyeballed my book.

He struggled to form his words, "N-No need... for fancy book learning... here." he reeked of alcohol.

I barely peered over the edge of my book, "I see, you're an audiobook kind of guy, huh?"

The drunk became confused and stuttered when he said, "Wh-What?"

I waited a moment, then looked over the rim of my book once more, "You were leaving."

It took a moment, but he said, "... Right, thanks." and staggered out the door.

Just as I was getting back to my book, the waitress came back and set my glass of water on the table with more force than necessary.

She cocked her hip, "Is there anything ELSE you'd like, SIR?" things were going to get dangerous.

I didn't want the hassle, I had to hurry before there was trouble. I closed my book after noting the page in my head and put it away. As I feared, before I could grab my glass of water, the trouble had come. She was on my lap in the blink of an eye and ran her hands all over me.

"Oh, it was you, baby!?" she blushed, "How long has it been since our paths last crossed?"

I needed to let her down easy, "Look..." I paused to quickly glance at her name tag, "Susan."

She strangled me with a hug, "Oh, you remembered my name, sweety!"

I narrowed my eyes, "Yeah, sure... Anyway, all I want is to drink my water."

She smiled, "Don't worry, as a woman, it's my job to know the needs of my man!" she said as she leaned in to kiss me.

I stood, dropping her on the floor, chugged my water, slapped down the payment, and said, "Thanks for the water."

I left and could hear her swear she'd get me next time. It was life experiences like these that really made me realize I only attracted the crazies. After paying for my water, I needed to get some funds. As I continued into town, the buildings became nicer the farther in I went. The rich lived in the center of town, which left the homeless to live in the slums on the outskirts.

The conditions had improved so greatly, one could mistake it for the world before it ended. I ignored all of it, for the bank was my true objective, but it was unfortunately too early for it to be open. A catnap was in order, and I rested against the wall, falling asleep instantly...

CHAPTER 8
SHADOW OF HER FORMER SELF

F41RW4T3R, T1M3 UNK0WN -- The Shadow
Diva observed the corruption around her with anger.

I sat at the table near the back of the train station
cafe and watched the worker ants. I tapped my fingernails
against the table and occasionally sipped my coffee. The
beans had been overused, muddy water from a well would
have tasted better. Though, the babbling of the mindless
drones would have made anything taste bad. All I wanted
was some peace and quiet.

The idiots walked by with stupid grins, the ones of
sheep. They pissed me off with the alienated expressions
they threw to everyone. Their smiles were masks that
covered their shadows, their true self. While everyone else
saw those stupid grins, I saw the darkness of their soul.

I hated them, just the sight of them sickened me. Their dishonesty corrupted the world around them. I struggled to turn it off, but it was everywhere. It raped every corner of my mind with its filthy, rotten touch. The hypocritical truth that I had come to realize cut deepest.

I focused into the crowd by accident, just by trying not to. The cashier's greed as she shorted every customer. His lust as he ogled her body, never the wiser. They thought they hid their darkness well, but people learned to ignore it in exchange for the same. I shuffled through the mass of sins and heard a man yelling into his phone.

The stench of his pride flowed from him like a bad cologne worn in excess. Mixed with it, the vilest of them all, the horrid odor of wrath burned my lungs. It always overwhelmed me, and I became conscious I was reading them. There was a job I was there to do, and it was time. I had spent a week scoping out the building across the street, the Word spoke highly of the goodies inside.

I stood and exited the cafe as I checked my watch. This job was easy to pull, I could just walk right, but where was the fun in that!? The hard way gave the thrill of being caught. As I was lost in thought, a man approached me, but I threw my dirty water in his face.

I knew what he wanted, "Take a cold shower..." I said as I walked past without batting an eye.

I had no interest in those scum. He was pissed and that was hilarious. On the street, I took one last look at the Cardigan building from the outside. It was tall, but tiny against the grey backdrop above. The building stood mighty against the turbulent sky.

I was caught off guard by the blonde idiot as he burst through the crowd.

He screamed as he ran past, "Wee!", but he abruptly stopped with an angry look on his face, "Hey, it's not fun if everyone's doing it!"

"You're the only one who's naked..." a man said.

The idiot cut him off, "Sir, stop!" he said with his hand held out, "This is between me and the forty-nine and a half ninjas! They're everywhere..." he said, shifting his eyes side to side, "Yeah, this guy knows what I'm talking about." and he pointed to Mr. Suave.

He thought for a moment, "Umm... This guy... looks like that guy who escaped from that mental institution for... umm... hamburgers. Yeah, that's it. I think they said he likes to get naked so he can direct traffic... ... He punches babies!"

The idiot ran off flailing his arms in the air as he screamed, "The men in white will never catch me!"

In the confusion, Mr. Suave snuck away, and I scrubbed the last ten seconds of my life from memory. I made my way to the side entrance for the deliveries and pickups. I passed the guard booth and the man inside didn't even notice me. He was watching an old black and white show on a tiny television. He was getting paid to do nothing.

With no resistance, I proceeded onward. I hid until the armored car showed up. Out stepped two sharply dressed men in suits, one black and bald, the other on the lean side with hair dyed red. The bald man was neatly dressed and constantly made sure his attire was flawless. The second man was sloppy, shirt untucked and his tie barely hung on.

Both wore the same pair of shades, but the similarities ended there. Something didn't seem right about them. They seemed less human than everyone else and corruption oozed out. Didn't matter, all I had to do now was shadow them, and I'd have what I came for. Mamma was about to score big and get that new pair of shoes!

Once inside, security was easy, and my prize was in sight. As I hung from the ceiling, I found myself pitted against the final stretch. Get down the hallway without being seen and I was golden. I couldn't believe all the loot I was seeing, it was like a mansion inside of a skyscraper. It was filled with so many priceless artworks...

I caught sight of a painting of a woman that hung below me. Upon closer examination, something wasn't right. I needed to fix it with a permanent marker. With a few quick strokes, I had drawn a mustache and beard on her as well as a few blacked out teeth. I loved to add my own contributions to the art community, especially if it puts dirty skanks in their place.

Just as I was about to drop down, a door opened and two men escorted out a woman with a bag over her head. She was handcuffed and wrapped in chains like she was a prisoner. They took the elevator, and the coast was clear.

Farther down the hallway, I got an uneasy feeling. I heard a voice and not the kind you should hear.

It reached out from every shadow and called me in. It pierced my brain, which caused me to stumble, and I barely caught a vase I had knocked over. The voice's words were unclear, too powerful. I stepped from the shadows, and the voice vanished like it always did. Though, that time it seemed somehow familiar to me.

I had made it without getting caught, and my prize awaited me. It was this fancy Faberge egg that was worth an arm and a leg. It had been in Russia for years and went missing after the Revelation Outbreak. It was priceless in this day and age, and finally, it was... gone!? Had I gotten the room wrong?

It was supposed to be right there... where that card was sitting. A calling card, with a single "X" printed on it. Some cocky, bitchass thief beat me to it, son-of-a-bitch! I was pissed, I was going to take the place for all it was worth. I looted anything that wasn't nailed down, because I wasn't leaving empty-handed.

Once I was carrying all I could, I headed back into the hallway. I may not have gotten what I had come for, but to rob the bitch blind felt like a public duty. As I stepped past the elevator, the doors opened, but I was met by a pair of guns.

"Well, shit." I said as I stepped back.

The two suits from outside and the woman who owned the place came out with a smug look.

"Whoa, lady! I didn't take the egg."

DEVIL INSIDE – THE MAN WITH CRIMSON EYES VOL. 1

"I know you didn't, but because of the other one, I had to step out of a very important meeting. These two have informed me of who you are, and what you are capable of, Shadow Diva, and your disguise is ridiculous." that bitch, my face was not a disguise, "Honestly, I couldn't care less, I only want what is mine returned to me."

"I work alone." I said defensively, "That X guy came and went before I even got here."

"Yes, I said as much already, but you have also stolen from me!" and she held out her hand.

I wasn't happy about it, and it showed on my face as I pulled the waist of my pants out and reached down into my panties. I pulled out a small sack that had a few jewels in it and placed it in the bitch's hand. She rolled her eyes as she shook her head with a sigh. Cunt thought she was better than me just because she had money. The redhead had gotten a little excited, but I couldn't read the bald one through his stoic expression.

I just smiled at her and said, "Got to keep the family jewels close to home." and I patted the front of my pants.

"Hand everything over." she said.

Since they had guns and asked so nicely, I did as they wanted. I reached into my many pockets and unloaded the contents on the table next to me. I had a few gold coins in my right pants pocket, one small gold mask I had put under my jacket, and a fancy dagger I had stuffed down the back of my pants. The sheath got caught on my belt as I removed it, and I nearly cut my ass. I had to wiggle my butt to get it loose.

I had a thin, flat bar of gold shaped like a card in a pocket inside my jacket, and a wad of silky cloth on the other side. I unzipped my pants and dropped trou to get to the stuff I had strapped to my thighs. I wore baggy pants on the job for a reason, a lot of reasons actually. Among some of the things I had strapped to my legs were a couple of candlesticks, some silverware, actually made of silver. An engraved compass, a silver flask, a tiara I had fastened over my thigh, and some gold tassel or something I wrapped around my leg.

I pulled my pants back up and pulled a handful of earrings and rings from my breast pockets. I reach up both my pant legs to remove a couple of small knives and took out the bracelets from under my arm sleeves. I lifted my shirt for the silver plate and hand mirror I had strapped to my stomach. On the backside of the strap, I had a decorative axe, I wrapped the blade first. I had several necklaces with assorted jewels around my neck.

Oh, and I had a cigarette case stashed in my bra, both sides, and they were a little sweaty. By the time I was done, their facial expressions conveyed confusion, surprise, and disbelief.

"What?" I shrugged, "As a professional courtesy, when I rob someone, I take them for all their worth. I only had one trip and had to make it count." I mumbled as I crossed my arms defensively.

"Hell!" the redhead said, "I'm surprised you didn't take the painting." and he pointed behind me.

"I tried... wouldn't fit in my pants." I said nonchalantly.

"Yeah, well, what about this?" he said as he reached for my neck.

He pulled out my locket attached to a gold chain, "That's mine, let go before you lose the hand."

"Leave it!" the high-class bitch said, "My family would never collect something so tacky."

"TACKY!" I was ready to cut the bitch, but I wasn't faster than bullets, so I backed down.

"I've already called the police. Get her moving!" she said in a demanding tone.

The two motioned me with their guns, "Move it." the bald one said, it was actually the first thing he had said. I looked back at all the loot as it sat on the red table runner embroidered with golden thread.

They nudged me and as they started to walk me away, I stopped, "Come on, we can work something out, right!?" I asked.

"I don't want to hear it!" she growled.

"Had to try!" and the three of them walked me out to the cops.

The bald goon whispered, "You may want to change before you get found out. Just a professional courtesy." but I had no idea what he was talking about.

The rich bitch had a smug smirk on her face as her two goons loaded me into the back of the cruiser. It had been so hard to keep the smile off my face, but playtime was over. The cops had been so distracted by their argument that they never once looked at me.

"Hey, Chapel!" the dumb one said.

I could hear the two talk as I wiggled in the back seat.

Chapel responded, "No, Trane." with a pissy attitude.

"But I haven't even asked you the question yet." he sounded disappointed.

"Shut up, Trane." and Chapel asked, "Lady, what's your name so we can start the paperwork?"

"Paperwork, we don't have any paperwork." Trane said.

"Trane, shut up!"

"But Chapel!?" he continued.

"Lady...?" he said as he turned to the back.

"Can I ask you my question, now?" Trane asked.

"Jesus Christ Trane, SHUT UP!" Chapel shouted and Trane got quiet, "Now, care to tell me where the woman went?"

Or at least that's how I imagined their conversation went, but I wouldn't know. I wasn't in the backseat for more than a few seconds. Inside, though, I suspected that the classy bitch was just realizing that I had duped her.

"All in all, today was a good haul." I said as I lifted the red table runner I had tied into a sack with the gold tassel. I threw it over my shoulder and walked away as I twirled the sack of gems on my finger. Once I had broken free, I snuck back in and robbed her a second time.

"The suckers always take their eyes off me." I smiled excitedly.

I was so happy, I couldn't contain myself. I would be riding the high of robbing that bitch for days...

CHAPTER 9
RENEGADE

"A long time after the French revolution, in a certain city, there was a lone man who fought for humanity and justice. However, "man" isn't entirely correct, this man was a salmon. This salmon-man gained a humanoid body, and with it, superpowers from a lab experiment involving radiation and a bacon cheeseburger. He was born into a majestic life in a lake somewhere in Canada, but his story was a sad one where he was taken from his wife and kids and subjected to cruel tests. Though, his heart is kind, and he uses his powers for the greater good despite humanity's cruelty.

His story is a heroic one, full of life, vigor, and fish, but this tale is not his. It is about a far less important man, who spends every waking moment of his life hammered out of his mind and provides no important contributions to the community. He spends his time gambling in bars, getting into fights, and well, just acting plain crazy on a regular basis. Only the brave venture near him and only the bravest challenge him. Somewhere, in a pub, this man tempts fate once more in a die-hard drinking game."

THE SQUEAKY CHAIR, FAIRWATER, THE 27TH -- The Silver Bullet sat on the wrong end of a do or die game of shots.

I sat back in my chair as I slowly swished whiskey in my shot glass. My company wasn't much to look at, they were rather displeasing actually. I had my cowboy hat pulled down over my eyes so they couldn't read any impending bluffs. They were a rough lot, dressed head to toe in leather and chains, clad in tattoos, and an odor that burned my nose. I lit up like a beacon in the fog, a long silver trench coat didn't blend with charcoal black jackets.

The only thing that really matched was my messy blonde hair that stuck out from under my hat. I should have been nervous, but the clatter and chatter made me itch for the brawl that always breaks out here.

Across from me sat a twitchy-eyed biker who slammed his meaty fist on the table, "Hurry up, boy, I ain't got all fuck'n day and don't you be think'n about chicken'n out. If you try to run, I'll cut your fuck'n balls off!" that's Willis, he was an impatient hothead with a penchant for collecting balls.

He was a drinking buddy, an acquaintance really, I've only drunk with him a couple of times, and he wasn't the losing type of gent. After his little display, the air grew tense, and I had my trigger finger tapping against the sawed-off holstered to my thigh. He was a violent guy, the ball cutting and all but caveman mentality and steroid-induced "episodes" weren't my concern. In the corner of my eye, I saw a certain troublemaker as he strolled into my territory like a stray cat that thought he owned the place. It had gotten me thinking it was time to get things rolling earlier than I wanted, but I loved the challenge of changing a plan on the fly.

I turned my attention back to the matter at hand, "Listen, Willis, I know chickens, and I ain't one of them. Now, why would I run, drink'n is my speci-alty?" and I raised my head just enough to look him in the eye from under the rim of my hat.

It was like a western standoff at high noon, and I gave a little smirk before I effortlessly threw back the shot in one gulp and slammed it down.

Willis's eye twitched a little before he smirked, "Damn, boy, you're good. Hey, Susan, get your sweet ass over here, now!" and he waved down the redhead across the room.

She was a waitress that worked in this bar if you could call it that, but I've always felt, the more run-down, the more laid back it was. Everyone knew who she was, but wouldn't as much as look at her, and for good reason. While she had a tight ass and decent rack, there was one major problem any fool could tell after he stepped one foot in the room. She was Willis's girl and castration pretty much summed it up rather nicely. Now, I was a man who admired the fairer sex, but even I wasn't crazy enough to ogle her in front of him.

Though I wouldn't want to brag about how great my peripheral vision was, that's all I'm saying. She floated across the room in her daisy dukes and flaunted her hips back and forth like the pendulum of a clock. Every man averted their eyes like Death just rode into town.

She stopped shy of the table and cocked her hips to the side, "What do you want, Willis? I'm busy!" she asked with a flustered attitude.

He grabbed her wrist and locked on like a vice grip. I wanted to shoot him on principle alone, but I waited to see how things played out.

"Lose the attitude or I'll beat some respect into you!" he said as he stared her down, "Get us another six rounds and make it snappy. Hurry and get your fine ass back here quick, you hear me, woman!?" he said as he released his grip.

"Yes..." she rubbed her wrist, and I could see the handprint as clear as day from behind my hat.

She walked away as I spotted a tear roll down her cheek, and my finger coiled all the more around my trigger. He slapped her ass, and I could see her swallow her pride as she bit her lip.

Willis pridefully watched her walk away. She had all but lost her former grace, and he was proud of himself for beating down her spirit.

He smirked, "A good ass on that one, wouldn't you agree, cowboy!?"

He was dumber than he looked, which was an accomplishment. He was looking for an excuse to start something, and he thought a trick like that would save his ass from the match.

It was easy to see through, "I have some integrity spiky..." I said to mock his mohawk, "My eyes don't wander." all lies, naturally.

"Smart man!" he was full of himself.

This is where things would've taken a turn for the worst, all because of her. You'd understand if you saw things the way I did. She was "his" girl, he was "protective" as you can imagine, and he watched her like a hawk. She passed the ninja on her return, drifting her eyes slightly toward him.

Willis's eye twitched like he was having an aneurysm, "I'll kill that shit." he snarled.

I grabbed his wrist, "She's your girl. She was taunting him, showing off what only a real man could have." it was stupid, but it was the first thing that came to mind.

Only an idiot would've believed that bluff, "Yeah, you're right!" he said with a smug grin.

The man was a fool beyond words, and luckily, my hat covered me laughing my ass off.

"You just saved that punk's life! Didn't think you were the merciful type." then he looked at my hand, "Oh, and get your hand off me!"

"Yeah..." I said, letting go, "I saved HIS life. I take my drink'n very seriously, and I'd rather not have blood spilled before I'm drunk enough to do it myself." and I paused, "But first, we need some drink'n music." I said as I stood up, but they reached for their guns, "Whoa, guys, I'm just going to the jukebox."

I lifted my leg to step over my chair and barely caught myself from falling by hopping on one foot. I walked to the jukebox, at least that's what I hope it looked like, because it sure as hell didn't feel like it. As I closed in, a cute blue-haired girl walked in anxiously through the backdoor. It was subtle, but I could tell she had a Japanese heritage from her facial markers.

Without a second thought, I stumbled into her, saved us from falling, and placed my hat in her hands as I wobbled away.

"Hey, sir, old onto me at, would ya, fine lass?" at least, I hoped that's what I said all with the smiling face of someone blinking during a snapshot.

I didn't stay to admire her confusion, I needed my music. As I braced myself on the jukebox, I browsed the selection of songs.

In the background, I heard a man say, "Hey, that's my hat?"

I ever so slightly looked over my shoulder and saw he was talking to the cute Asian girl. I quickly covered my face and began whistling to blend in. Luckily, she was the silent type, he wasn't getting anything on me. Too many variables were going to cause things to go awry, I needed to act fast. I jabbed my finger at the first button that looked good.

Unfortunately, I missed horribly and stumbled from the jukebox before slamming into the backdoor. It flew open, causing Willis and his boys to grab their guns, thinking I was running away. My grasp on the doorknob and my foot on the lip of the door frame had saved me. As I hung, I saw a group of men with blue glowing needles sticking out them. They were alive, I could see their ragged breathing.

They'd been paralyzed, "Now, that's not something you see every day!" I muttered, "Why are five grown men laid out flat like porcupines in an alley when they could be in here getting laid out by the hard stuff!?"

They were unresponsive, can you believe it, the nerve of some people, how rude!? I didn't have time to mess with druggies and pulled myself back in, forgetting the entire ordeal. I made my way back to the jukebox, and all the guns were returned to their holsters. I found the button again and pressed it with great satisfaction. I waited for the good times to roll... but they weren't rolling!

I pressed it repeatedly with increasing force, only for the same outcome. I slapped it around, kicked it below the belt, and threw in a few curses for good measure. At some point, the bartender had walked over and started spewing some trash.

Something like, "It wasn't plugged in, and I knew that." hell, he had the gall to say, "You're the reason I have to unplug it every day." I think.

Truth be told, I had stopped listening somewhere around the... I wasn't sure. At this point, the bartender could have been in my imagination for all I knew.

I'd had enough, so I grabbed a bar stool and screamed, "Okay jukebox, that's how you want to play this game, is it? That's fine by me!"

"Now, you see, this man lacked civilized manners, whom for a lack of a more accurate description, was a total idiot. More than a few screws were loose, and he made the dullest tool in the shed look like an astrophysicist. He made the staff of loony bins check themselves in and therapists seek therapy. His idiocy was only made worse by his extreme love for the sauce, and strangely, chickens. "

I swung the stool into the jukebox window, breaking it into large shards and half a stool.

I turned and pointed dramatically to the closest person, a very confused man... or one ugly ass woman and yelled, "This is all your fault, and I am going to violently take my anger out on you. If you don't understand, just ask him." I said, pointing to the man-thing next to him.

From the look on his face, I could only assume that "other guy" was in my head... or maybe he was real and the first guy was in my head. Didn't matter, because by the time he turned back, I had already used the distraction to strap on my army helmet.

"What? That's just a bar stool." he said in confusion.

"Don't sass me, BOY!" I screamed as I laid him out flat with a left hook.

I turned my sights to Willis and his boys as I charged head first at them. Literally, diving at them like a battering ram soaring like a majestic eagle. I missed and fell flat onto the table, breaking it, and flung everything to the floor.

I quickly recovered and screamed, "Battle Royale!" as I shook intensely while throwing my fists into the air.

An awkward silence filled the room before all-out chaos broke loose, and I began dancing like a madman on an impulse. I weaved in and out of the individual fights that made up the mayhem in its entirety.

A hand on my shoulder quickly spun me around, and another sent the front of my face to meet the back of it, "Damn it, boy! I knew you'd try this shit!"

I stumbled into the bar and Willis charged after me, but I threw my finger up to symbolize I needed a second.

Strangely enough, he stopped, and I looked to the bartender, "Hey, you, give me a bottle of your finest shine, good sir, and a beer for your cow." I said with a raised lip and a haphazard salute.

The bartender halfheartedly obliged and handed me a bottle of moonshine from below the counter, probably out of shock, like an automated reflex. I chugged it, continuously motioning Willis for a moment. As I downed the last drop, I shattered the jar over his head. He didn't take kindly to the head trauma, but before he could recover,

I repeatedly rammed my knee into his nasal cavity. He broke free shortly after and swung his fists wildly.

I flowed like water, evading each punch with ease, but it only served to intensify his rage. I waited for an opening and landed a roundhouse to his face and flipped him over a table. As he slowly recovered, I reached into my trench coat and pulled out a rather large red cloth, it was silky smooth! I began taunting him, he the bull and I the matador as I kept him on his toes for the next couple of seconds. I used the cloth to throw off his perception of his surroundings until he went into a blind rage.

Desperate to get his hands on me, he charged with open arms, and I sidestepped. As the cloth slid over him, he crashed headfirst into the jukebox. As he passed out, I yelled out, "Ole!" and to my surprise, the jukebox came on.

"Yeah, I finally got it to work!" I screamed in excitement.

My victory was short-lived, as the bartender sent me flying out the front door and face first into the dirt.

"Don't come back until you can pay your tab and for the damages!" he shouted, slamming the door.

I rolled around, holding my face in pain while I screamed, "What horrible service! I'm coming back later today, you hear me, I'll be back!"

Then I heard clucking as my pet chicken ran to me from under the stairs.

"Oh, Fuji, that's where you've been. You're my wingman, why weren't you backing me up!?"

He cocked his head and pecked at the ground, "What, it's Sally, again!?" I said in shock, "Man, I told you she ain't worth it." but he ignored me, "What?! You say you love her? Fool, she's just using you for your manly feet. That woman has serious issues with feet. Break it off before you get hurt!"

An unfamiliar voice spoke out, "Having girl troubles!? Can I help!?"

"Oh, Fuji, you mock me because I care!?" I said with a heartfelt tear.

The voice spoke again, "No, good sir, over here."

I looked with a blank expression, and standing over me was a humanoid salmon with a monocle and suit. An all too familiar awkward silence drifted between us as a tumbleweed fluttered by.

The salmon raised its hands, "I know what you're thinking. A talking man-fish, it's going to eat the children! Don't be alarmed, I am only here to help you and your fine feathered companion."

I tilted my head in confusion, "Why would I be alarmed?"

The salmon tilted his head in a similar fashion, "Wait, you're not afraid of a talking fish?"

"Oh, sweet mother of someone else's god! A talking fish! Why didn't you tell me sooner!?" I screamed as I pulled out my two sawed-off shotguns and blasted the ever living shit out of it.

The fish-man flopped around on the ground for a while. I think he was milking the whole fish thing a little much. It was only funny for the first couple of seconds. Once he stopped moving, my eyes slowly crept to the left, to the right, back to the left, to the right again, and then, once more each way for good measure. I began dragging the dead fish-man off into the sunset with Fuji at my side as I whistled a cheery tune...

CHAPTER 10
THE WOMAN IN PURPLE

CLEARCREST, THE 27TH -- Little Red rode high in the dangerous sky as she ventured toward her goal.

Planes were expensive, but the only way between the Hellgates. Their protection didn't extend past the city limits, and it was dangerous enough inside them. In the Abyss, there is no safety from the monsters, only luck got you through the skies. The government was proud of their toys, but they were as effective as a broken condom.

It was nerve-racking to say the least, but a goal kept me in my skin. The only thing that was more stressful than flying through a storm of death with hungry monsters was the kid sitting across from me crying. By habit I was a loner, it was better that way, fewer attachments. However, this little girl was shaking like a leaf. Her mother was sleeping, but she was frightened out of her mind.

My stuffed rabbit was something I couldn't let go of, a security blanket. It had been so long that I couldn't remember why I held it so tightly. There was a nostalgic, calming effect that it had on me, but she needed its help more. I used funny faces as I made the rabbit dance for the little girl. At first, her fear rejected my attempts, but I eventually got a smile out of her.

She was a sweet girl, and we spent the trip laughing, and we both forget why we were so afraid. We hopped around cities before we made it to our final destination. From the terminal, we went our separate ways, and I never saw her again. Once outside, the air was cold and leaves rustled across the ground. It was fall, they were changing on the trees and floating on the breeze.

I referenced pictures from the articles and tried to find the crime scene, but it wasn't easy. It was hard to tell the redacted locations, the landscape was my only clue. I walked aimlessly for hours, interacting with people wasn't my idea of a good time, avoiding them was easier. Night was coming soon, the sun was setting, but a slight orange glow remained. It was all that could be seen from behind the blanket of clouds.

As I watched the leaves float, I walked alongside a chain-link fence. The air was chilly, everything was lonely, but at the same time peaceful. I found myself passing a basketball court, and a few kids were playing. The fence was cold and rough as I hooked my fingers on it. As I pressed against the fence, my thoughts were lost while I watched the ball bounce, and the kids were somehow having fun.

It was bizarre, how could they forget the world and have fun? They couldn't have been more than fourteen, surely, they were old enough to know. Yet, there they were, a simple game made them forget their worries. I leaned harder against the fence without being sure why. Was it a desire to be closer, to be a part of it and forget?

I must have looked odd standing there, without knowing it, they began watching me. Strange how at that moment that simple chain-link felt like a prison, a window that taunted me. The way their eyes looked at me, the way they watched me, it made me uncomfortable. I stepped back quickly and drew away from the freedom in that window. With the straps of my backpack in hand, I pulled my arms in tight.

As I walked away, the freedom dangling behind me slipped away. I focused on the articles and found a graveyard with thousands of tombstones lying in a row. It was littered with all things that had come there to die. I saw a dump, a place to forget the dead or broken. There were old, decrepit cars and a bus rusting away.

The graveyard had a terrible feeling to it, but beyond it, rested the warehouse. The place where the girl was murdered, and the place where my answers waited. The walk from the graveyard was short, and the feeling of the restless dead was eerie. The warehouse had been locked up tight by the police, limiting my options. Before I could accomplish the task at hand, there was the matter of breaking in.

Night soon fell, but thankfully, I was petite for a girl my age. My strength would have never gotten me in, but my size was my trump card. There was a small opening, and I threw my backpack through before following. Slipping through on my side was easy enough, being tiny had its perks. The concrete and metal chilled my leg and dirtied my clothes.

Once through, I dusted myself off and adjusted my sweat jacket. I picked up my backpack and searched the warehouse for the spot where she was murdered. It was mostly open, which made it easy to find the blood. Once everything was set up, I was ready for the seance to begin. I focused on her, clearing my mind of everything else.

I heard the wind rattle the glass as rain beat against the roof. I heard the whispers, the voices of the dead faded in and out. Shifting through the voices in the sea of sorrows was hard. The Revelation Outbreak was to thank for that, billions of people died. The outbreak left an uncountable amount lingering in our world.

For every soul unable to move on, there was an unheard voice screaming out. With the chance to be heard in a world that doesn't know you're there, you'd take it. You'd shout until they answered. They yelled out to be heard, calling for my help. Even if it hurt to push them aside, there was no other way to finish what I had come to do.

The screaming in my head hurt, but then she appeared to me. The candles flickered as she pressed against the veil. It was like stepping to a window in the darkness. The closer you are, the easier to see through, but only to be seen by the one on the other side. Pulling a spirit into our world was dangerous, but luckily, she didn't need to cross over.

A tiny blue flame birthed before me and slowly drifted. It was weak and dimly gave off a soft glow. Her soul was fresh, she was still raw, I came into this knowing that. She hadn't been dead long enough to manifest her will, it was like being there with your mind asleep. A person takes time to adapt, adjust to being a soul with no body.

She was twice the size of the average flame of a lighter. A sky blue flame with rolling waves rising to the top. The smoke trail was like a tail flowing off the top that gave her a teardrop shape. As I watched her soul float, I entered a hypnotic trance and made the connection. It was all fuzzy at first, like dreams, most details were hazy, but some as clear as day.

I began seeing as she had seen, the feelings, the smells, it was a rush. She burned with desire, she was in heat, and on the hunt for a man. All her senses were being overwritten by her lust, one thought was on her mind. There were flashes of men, she had a type, strong jaw, and a tight butt. I couldn't judge her, people tend to do what they want when the world ends.

That all changed one night she was out looking, mingling on the dance floor. She joined the crowd, grinding on the men, and shooting them dirty glances. All the men were aggressive, but she was the animal. They were chunks of meat to please her. Suddenly, she was hit by a red-hot burning desire and her heart fluttered.

She scanned the room looking for something, and that's when she saw someone sitting in the back of the bar. The figure moved closer, and like magnets, they were drawn together. The figure never came into focus, but I could tell it was a woman, which wasn't her type. Her emotions were conflicted, she'd never been with a woman, but something about her was different. She feared it, she was flooded with confusing thoughts, the wanting, needing.

They locked lips and embraced without hesitation, as naturally as shaking hands. They burned with passion, a fire had been lit inside her. Playing and taunting each other, the other woman chased away the men. It wasn't long before they left the bar, the strange woman led her by hand. Everything became fuzzy, all she could think about was this woman.

Without seeing how, they were at the warehouse, her feet dragged. She was afraid, but at the same time, her heart ached at the thought of letting go. Once inside, they didn't waste time shedding their clothing, and she laid down. She spread her legs inviting the mysterious woman in, wanting her so badly. Their skin melded, flesh blurred the boundaries between reality and fantasy.

It wasn't long before she melted, the other woman knew all the right spots. She felt ecstasy and the feeling swelled inside her, but pleasure turned to pain. It was dark, I couldn't see more than she had. Her nails broke off as she dug her fingers into the concrete. Her abdomen twisted until the flesh ripped apart and blood splattered.

All the muscles in her body tightened, her eyes felt like they would explode from her head. The crunching sounds of bones echoed as her legs twisted around. She tried to scream, but her mouth flooded with blood, she couldn't breathe. After falling back lifelessly, her body twitched as her final moments slipped away. The last thing she saw was the mysterious woman walking away, dragging one of her legs behind her.

The vision stopped, and I wasn't any closer than I had been before. I had no clue as to how far they had walked, it had faded from her memory. More possibly, it was kept from her memory, that something prevented it from being created in the first place. There was no way of knowing whether or not it was the person I had been looking for. It could have been any number of things, human or monster, but I wasn't sure they were that different.

Rage was the least of what I was feeling inside me. I had nothing to go on, everything was too fuzzy. It was a dead end, but she floated past me. Her soul began drifting like she was leading me. She could lead me, why hadn't I remembered that?

I gathered my things and followed her, but she couldn't leave the warehouse. When a soul is released from its body, it becomes tethered to the location. It is generally confined to the boundaries of a structure or a plot of land. I knew how to tether her soul to myself, but I couldn't remember. I focused, but the harder I tried to recall, the further it slipped away.

I remembered a soul tether was simple to perform, but the words wouldn't come to me regardless of effort. To focus, I rubbed my thumb against my ring, it was my catalyst. I looked at it and became hypnotized by the blue light reflecting off of it. When I blinked, I could feel the soul tethered to me. I didn't remember doing it, which was weird.

I had done it wasn't important. So, I let the girl's soul lead me to wherever she wanted to go. We stepped out into the rain and I followed her light...

CHAPTER 11
STRIP CLUB SHOWDOWN

CRIMSON FLAMES, BEFORE THE SLEEPER ATTACK, THE 27TH -- The Black Dragon, in shock, remembered the events leading up to her dead eyes.

We spent the night partying, or rather I did, someone was a party pooper. Being without any good alcohol was bad enough, so we ignored the stick in the mud. Hours went by with nothing to show for our efforts, not that it was hard to wait for something to come to you. Eventually, I found myself sitting down, sulking next to the stick. One thing led to another, and I found myself standing over a lifeless corpse.

I looked into the woman's cold, dead eyes, and it filled me with such emotion. I couldn't save her, that was on me. It was hard to look at her twisted and contorted body. How had he done it with a single touch? What kind of power was capable of such a feat?

It was like a second person was trying to crawl out from inside her. I wasn't letting him get away with it. This woman, this club, it stopped there, even if I had to do it unarmed. He would never give me time to get my swords, so I had to make do. I hoped his power was limited to touch.

I thrust my fist into my open hand, pumping myself up for the fight. There may have been six of him, but there was one of ME!

"You dare harm innocent people!? You shall be punished, and as a man, it's my duty to put an end to your devilish deeds." I removed the master remote from my pocket, "Let's end this!" and I got the music blasting and the lights pulsing.

"You should have stayed out of this!" one of them screamed, and another yelled, "I've already seen your ice power, you can't surprise us!" they finished each other's sentences like they thought with one mind.

"Ice...?" I said, "... Not me. No ice powers here."

"Don't fuck with me! Sleepers only get one power!"

"True, but it's still no." I said, removing my jacket.

It was too constricting and hindered my mobility. I held a dead stare as I raised my fists and took my stance as I contemplated the best method of attack against this strange, new enemy. If I couldn't touch him, I needed a weapon and decided to grab a bar stool and held it by one of the legs. It was perfect for now, it gave me a way to attack while being defensive. I'm not one to attack first, but their rush solved that.

"We'll fucking kill you!" they screamed in unison.

I swung the stool out and went full circle, bashing some heads. One recovered quicker than the others and came at me. I flipped the stool around, grabbing it by the seat and put the legs around his torso. I gripped the seat hard and spun it like a steering wheel. I took him right off of his feet and to the floor.

Another got a lucky shot in from behind, broke a bottle over my head. It was quite the look on his face when it did nothing but shatter. I kicked him in the gut and flipped him over the bar. As I recovered my stance, the rest wildly flailed, hoping to grab me. It was too risky, so I ran.

I ripped the stool apart and threw the seat at them. I used the wooden legs to get through safely. As I turned, I unleashed a volley of attacks. With the stool legs, I played them like the crash cymbals of a drum set, smacking the bones closest to the surface, knuckles, wrists, elbows, etc... It wasn't as effective as I had hoped, they were just copies after all.

My eyes could spot a fake a mile away, but these guys were pretty durable. I had to pull out the big guns for them. I ran to the stage and charged at the stripper pole. Under normal circumstances, one of these wouldn't budge, but when a couple hundred pounds of raw muscle come crashing on you, you tend to give. They were short bars mounted only on the floor, making it the perfect length for a bow staff.

Now, I had ranged attack, and I smacked a couple of piñatas. It was going well until one snuck up behind me. I blocked with the pole and he swung a fire axe at me. When the first swing failed, he kept going at it until he cut in. I kicked him away and took a quick glance at the pole. I could still use it but not as a staff.

With my knee, I broke it into two shorter poles. I smashed his head between the two bars and kicked him back. Their new lengths made them like swords. I could do it, but I wasn't one for dual wielding, so I held them together like a greatsword. Since they weren't real, I didn't need to hold back and went for the kill.

The one I hit exploded into light and zipped off like fireflies, but with five more, there was no time to be confused. I swiped the feet out from under the next and tried to stab the poles into him while he was on the floor. However, another kicked them just hard enough for me to miss. He jumped up and kicked me back, but he missed with the second kick.

He swung his fists, but I brushed them away with ease. A different one kicked the poles from my hands, and I was thrown on the defense. It was hard to avoid, but I held my own. I had taken them too lightly, but I'd never been one to take personal danger too seriously. In all honesty, if I messed up one time, I'd die, and that would probably, ya know, be pretty bad.

There had been a lot of risks, but without a weapon, I had to take more. Two weapons were given to me by the gods, and while they weren't sharp, they did pack a punch.

I kept light on my feet and pulled my arms close to my core. Aiming for their weak points, I focused on brief contact and hoped his power couldn't activate quickly. Deflecting attacks while creating openings to strike back was no easy task.

I lunged in, putting my fist into a copy's face and laid him out flat. I was hoping the others had his glass jaw too. The next one came and I brought him down in a similar fashion. However, the next fight didn't have the odds in my favor and I bolted. I ran toward a wall, ran up, and flipped back over them.

As I landed, I knocked one away and pushed two into the wall. When they bounced back, I knocked one down, snapped the other's neck, and he became energy. It was like twisting a pillow, the copies were durable but strangely fragile too. A well-placed roundhouse finished the one getting up off the floor. For the next, I jumped off the wall for extra power and punched his lights out, literally.

It was lucky that I had gotten them down to two so quickly, and I had a plan to wrap it up. I still had the master remote, the ace up my sleeve. I walked toward them as they grouped together, it had worked so well for them until now. I got close, pulled out the master remote, and turned out the lights. They were blind, but just because they couldn't see me didn't mean I couldn't them.

I snuck behind them and took them out. I turned the lights on and looked around to make sure I was alone. The club was empty except for me, and there wasn't a moment to waste. I collected my swords from my room and strapped them to my hip. As I came back down, there was still one thing left to do, the most important.

I pulled down one of the drapes from the wall and laid it over the woman on the floor. I hadn't the time for a proper burial, but the least I could do was show her respect. I knelt next to her, closed my eyes, and said a little prayer.

"May the gods guide your soul so you may find peace." and after a moment of silence, I stood.

With my coat in hand, I ran out the front door with a smile on my face. My blood hadn't been pumping like that in a long time. I noticed the snow falling from the sky, it was strange, I didn't feel the cold anymore. As I went to leave, I saw a kid shivering something awful. He needed my coat more than I did.

"Hey, kid!" I said, startling him, "You're gonna catch a cold dressed like that, ya know. Here, take this!" and I put my jacket around him, then smiled.

The kid had looked at me like I was crazy as I ran off. I had no idea why, though. More importantly, I need to move fast before the city got blown up by a certain hot head...

CHAPTER 12
HELP ME, DOC!

You killed me!.....It was an accident!.....It was murder!
.....I tried.....You succeeded!.....

FAIRWATER, THE 27TH -- The Angel of Silence slept in her bed but violently tossed and turned.

I awoke in a cold sweat, the visions were getting worse. I curled up on the bed, wrapping my arms around my legs. The tears wouldn't stop, it hurt so bad. No matter how hard I suppressed it, the crazy always got through. I couldn't take it, I couldn't sleep, and I couldn't put my useless hands to work. I feared the unholy images that burned their way into my mind.

I looked at my clock, it was nearly eight and already dark. I had gotten some sleep, but it wasn't enough. It was that fear that kept me from sleeping, and I didn't want to feel the terror anymore. There was no way I was going back to sleep after that. With my heart pounding in my throat, I'd be lucky to calm down.

I spent the better part of an hour trying to relax, but it had no effect on my racing heart. My nerves were still rattled. I wasn't going back to sleep. I had no hobbies, no friends, nothing to occupy my time, but I was good at one thing. After getting some sleep, maybe if I begged them, they'd let me get back to work. I got dressed and headed for the hospital, taking the well-lit paths.

This city was dangerous, worse than before the Event, and the police were powerless. When the world darkened, the faithless turned to darker things. While few turned to God, others fell to their desires. Thugs outnumbered the police one hundred to one. The city was bad off, not enough of anything except water, electricity, and air to go around.

The rich hoarded everything, while people on the streets died from hunger on the inside and cold on the outside. I had little more than they did, a small apartment and clothes full of holes. To them, a little was a dark temptation haunting their minds. One day if their faith ever faltered, there would be nothing to hold them back from the promise of safety in return for their humanity. All around I saw men, women, and children with that look in their eyes, they were close to the edge.

To them, God had abandoned us, but they had only become blind to his light. It was something that tore me up every time I saw it. That's why, if I could save these people, even if only one by one, I could open their eyes to his light again. If they were too far gone, I'd try harder, no one was beyond his light. It's just hard to find when the world doesn't want you to see it.

Everyone has their own trial, and even if the world had ended, I could still see the Lord's light where the sun used to be. My faith was stronger than ever, and I was able to walk his righteous path. His light shielded me from the darkness in the world, and I arrived at the hospital safely. It was busy as usual, I was sure they'd let me come back to work, they had to. We were short-handed before, they couldn't help all the wounded people, and even my useless hands could do something.

I made it to the receptionist's desk before she tried to stop me. I darted away from her, slipping past through a crowd, but two guards were waiting for me. As panic set in, I tried to rush past them, but they dragged me to the receptionist kicking and screaming.

"You were told to go home and rest!" she snarled, "They knew you'd try this. They warned me you would." I wanted to say something, but she wouldn't have listened, "They said we could kick you out the door if you resisted." and she leaned in, "Please, resist!" she was mean today.

I turned around with tears rolling down my cheeks, it hurt me so deeply. All I ever tried to do was help, and I was stopped at every turn. Was helping so wrong!? I walked over to a chair and sat down to stop my tears, I didn't want them freezing to my face in the cold. As I sat there trying to calm myself, that question went through my head over and over.

I heard the receptionist arguing with someone, "Sir, you will have to wait just like everyone else!" she glared, she was intimidating.

"I can't. This is an emergency!" he yelled.

"An emergency, huh!?" she said with an attitude, "Have you lost most your blood from severed limbs, having a heart attack, or even dying of a disease no one's heard of!?"

"I've got a date with a hot piece of tail in half an hour!" he said, completely serious, "And she's not a whore! Do you have any idea how hard it is to find a piece of high-quality ass like that, let alone one that hasn't turned to selling her body for money? Not that I'm insinuating only women do it, I had an old drunk guy offer me something a couple of hours ago that I'd never heard of, and that's a feat. So, it takes all kinds, but if you haven't notice lady, the world's ended, and I've got a date!"

"Boy!" she said, pulling her hand back to smack him, "If you don't get out of here, security is going to give you a real reason to be here!"

"But my penis!" he pleaded.

"Wh-What!? His pe-pe-pe…" I screamed in my head.

The receptionist had a different reaction and tried to climb over the counter.

He was too quick and jumped back screaming, "Do you know who you're dealing with!? I'm Braydon Darko, and if I EVER get superpowers, you are SOOOOO going to regret this!"

He saw the security guards coming for him and his attitude quickly changed. He scurried away at the mere sight of them with his tail between his legs. If he was distracting them, maybe I could sneak past, but that went out the window when he saw me.

He was always causing trouble around town, nothing bad, but he annoyed everyone. So, when he looked my way, I panicked.

"Doctor!" he yelled, "Doc, I have to talk to you!"

I didn't know what to do, he must have remembered my face. The first thing I could think of was to hide. I took off through a crowd of people and hid behind a worn down magazine rack. I was sure I'd lost him, and as soon as I thought the coast was clear...

"Doc, why are you on the floor?" and I turned to see him standing behind me.

I was so surprised, I almost wet myself. I fell over trying to get away, and by the time I stood, he was standing in front of me.

"I need your advice Doc.." he said, unzipping his pants.

My hand reacted on its own and grabbed the first thing it could to protect my eyes. I grabbed a magazine and barely held it out in time to obstruct, i-i-IT!!!

Strangely, he silently looked at the magazine, and I heard glass breaking, followed by the words, "Yep, that did it!" he zipped his pants and hu-hu-hugged me, I felt faint,

"Thank ya, Doc! You always know how to help a guy out. You would not believe the things the little guy gets stuck in." and he ran away.

All my blood had rushed to my face, and I fell to my butt dizzy. It took a moment for my heart to stop pounding, and as my clarity came back, I happened to look at the magazine cover. On it was a picture of a very large man with reddish orange hair and a big bushy beard. Of course, I instantly recognized him, it was the greedy glutton and he had his money-grubbing grin on as always. Just because it had his face on it, the magazine felt unsanitary, and I felt dirty.

After washing my hands under water hot enough to scald flesh, I left the hospital. There was no reason to go home and work was out of the question.

I heard the words, "Hey, bitch!" shouted from behind me, followed by a sharp pain on the back of my head, then, nothing…

CHAPTER 13
THE HOTEL SHUFFLE

ELSEWHERE IN FAIRWATER, THE 27TH -- The Gobbler held dearly the moment of peace which desperately tried to slip through his fingers.

Alas, it was a fleeting moment, and the burdens of my life pulled me back down. I closed my eyes, taking a deep breath as I tried to grab onto one more second of peace. I let out a sigh, it was back to work, and the moment was forever gone in the strenuous thought that followed. I reached into the breast pocket of my flannel shirt and pulled out a small metallic disc of my own creation, patent pending.

I activated the recorder and a holographic projection of my magnificent self appeared.

I quickly organized my words with great skill and spoke carefully, "My name is Andrew Inferious, and not too long ago I was an important piece on the board that is the world I had hidden my status as a player quite well, but now, I'm hiding from the people who worked beside me. Someone has set me up, leaked top-secret information, and made sure it was only data I had access to. Naturally, I was suspected, because I'm awesome. During my search, I have found something that disturbed me, and I've been to the dark corners of the internet.

Through all my digging, I keep finding one thing, a single "X", the culprit's calling card. I thought it would be bad if Benson and the Collective got my data, but now... Now, someone out there has it, an unknown variable to the equation. Worst of all, they have the skill and know-how to rival my own. It's difficult to admit, but there is someone out there as good as me, except... THEY got caught."

I was amused at the thought, and my tone became lighter, "That's alright. I'm not surprised. I figured this would happen someday, and I've taken steps to ensure my preservation." I said, grinning happily, "Besides, I was getting bored being the good guy. I suppose I can play the villain for a while."

I had not finished my monolog yet, and I was quite enjoying too. I was interrupted and my train of thought ruined when I glimpsed a shimmer across the street. On the rooftops, across from the hotel, from behind the rain, I spotted a scope lens. I rolled from my chair to the floor. A bullet pierced my favorite coffee cup. It had an "I Heart Grandma" with a digital pulsing heart that lit up red.

The glass shards scattered across the floor as footsteps stormed the hall. They had tracked me, an SAS hit squad, but I was prepared! I activated the secondary device in my watch, my design, patent pending. The sniper would have x-ray scopes, and standard vision gear, night, heat, etc... Mine would scramble their tech, and they'd be in the dark, literally, as I turned off my lamp.

I stood, closing the blinds with my grinning silhouette fading into the shadows. Into the darkness, like a ninja, my presence became one with the room. The soldiers breached the door. They were tightly huddled, rotating in a circle as if chained at the hip. They scanned the room with their assault rifle mounted flashlights. I knew their formations, foresaw their tactics, I wrote most of them myself.

The leader raised his fist, the squad halted, and he whispered on the coms, "No visual, he's gone, sir." but no response came, "Damn, equipment's down!" and they split up to continue their search.

They would never find me, I was like the wind, "Uh-oh!" I thought as crumbs fell from the ceiling. The soldier below me brushed them away. The fool had no clue I was lurking above them. My skill was matched by no one... "Oops!" and my butt cheeks clenched.

More crumbs fell, but this time he didn't let it pass. Through my specially modified goggles, I saw him look me dead in the eyes. He wasn't going to leave it to chance and slowly raised his gun. I couldn't let him alert the others. I grabbed him, pulling him up before they saw me. On his way up, he dropped his gun, alerting them.

They mumbled, "Where is he? We're not alone!"

The remaining three were on guard, focused where he'd been standing. I quietly knocked him unconscious and threw him across the room to draw their attention. They turned their backs to the window, and I slid down before it like a spider. Outside a spotlight shined through the window, and the last thing they saw was my menacing shadow.

First, they tried their pathetic bullets, but they failed. I took them down with speed and skill, and they were supposed to be elites. They were nothing against my training and genius! One by one, I took them down until only I remained in the darkness. I cracked the door, and I scouted the hallway for more losers.

I scoffed at their hubris but was met by a man as I stepped out. He had dashingly amazing charisma, and roguishly handsome, good looks with a strong, bushy beard sporting a red-orange hue. I realized this sexy beast was none other than my studly reflection in a mirror. I rolled up the sleeves of my flannel shirt and adjusted my collar. I shut the door behind me, and headed downstairs, my plan was in action.

"You realize I'm going to have everyone assassinated once this is over, right?" I boasted from safety around the corner.

I had hit the next wave of enemies lurking in the lobby.

"That's right, fatass. Make threats while you hide like a coward!" a man laughed, "Even your threats have someone else doing your dirty work!"

"There are payments to make and bribes to issue. That's a lot of hard work I'll have you know! I also have to move the money around after hacking your bank accounts so you're the ones paying for and covering up your own assassinations. It's exhausting!" I hoped they'd appreciate the hard work involved.

"It's a wonder you ever got caught doing your own dirty work." he mocked and that made me so angry, I was going to make him overpay for his death.

Using my badass ninja skills and a shard of a mirror, I conveniently found on the floor, I kept track of their movements. Their commander motioned and their formation spread out. One-half covered the other as they took the stairs. They climbed to the second floor, never knowing I had stood in that exact spot. They were going to be easy and it amused me.

My laughter echoed, concealing my location. The leader took a moment, and they disappeared upstairs. Three remained on the first floor, none the wiser I was already behind them. Like a predator leaping from the shadows, I dropped between them, unleashing lightning quick strikes defeating two. My brilliant detective skills deduced the third soldier was a girl!

She spun around, I took her gun and threw it across the room. Girls meant one thing, boobies, woohoo! She pulled out her combat knife and attacked with decent skill.

She wasn't half bad, it was shame about her handicap, though.

"Silly woman!" I smiled as I waved my finger, "Girls can't fight."

I whipped out my athema and sliced off her protective gear, and took some of her uniform too. Her girly reaction made it all too easy to take her knife and corner her. I slowly inched toward her, hopping on my feet in quick, short, but repetitive steps as I crept forward with a devilish grin. I held my hands out, and my fingers wiggled like they had a life of their own.

I began laughing maniacally, "Mwhahahahaha! Let me ask you. Do you like tentacles and school-issued swimsuits!?"

A look of horror and dread took root in her eyes as she screamed and escaped under my grasp, but I grabbed her shirt. The cuts previously made caused it to rip off, revealing her full glory... "The hell is this!?" my brain screamed in disgust.

She was wearing some unsexy, standard issue sports bra that was more like a shirt. In my mental breakdown, she had grabbed her gun and bolted outside.

"Oh well..." I shrugged, "Two more to go, but what a letdown."

I climbed the stairs enthusiastically, but super stealthily! I found them in a storage room, and heard them reading my little note, "IT IS TOO LATE TO TURN BACK." They thought it was funny until I spun the subordinate around and broke his glass jaw. It was the unit leader and myself remaining for the final showdown. Taking cover for someone of my skill and highly trained physique was child's play.

"How'd you get past my men, fatass!" he threw insults as he searched.

I scoffed, "I am not fat, I am just more huggable for greater pleasure!" I nodded my head, "And your men?" I asked with a raised brow, "By punching them, naturally! They certainly were a disappointment." I sighed, "Four and not one managed to touch me, plus, one was only a girl!"

He fell for my trap and aimed for my voice, "I'll kill you!" but I took his gun from behind.

"I wonder," I said, plucking the rifle from his grasp, "if you will?" and I threw it away, "My doctor tells me I need more metal in my diet, but I guess I won't be eating this lead!"

I thrust my palm into his chest, throwing him back, but he thought he could match my brilliance with his combat knife.

"I hope you fight better than a girl!" I jested.

He spouted nonsense, "You're going to pay for your betrayal, traitor!"

I grinned, "Shh, don't tell anyone!" I said with my finger to my mouth.

Charging at him was the best move, and a simple lunge of his knife was all he could muster. I grabbed his wrist, stopping the attack, but he dropped it to his off hand. He aimed for my neck, but I predicted his novice attack. I grabbed him by the vest with all my strength. I slammed him into the wall, and he dropped the knife.

I dragged him across the wall, tearing up the wallpaper and destroying the shelving. It was hard to lift a full grown man, but his weight worked against him when I dropped him through a table.

I sighed and muttered to myself, "I had hoped you'd provide a challenge, but I didn't even break a sweat. I let you use your knife too!" I walked to him and stomped on his neck, "But I guess you were just a generic enemy and not a mini-boss after all!" and I kicked him unconscious.

I nonchalantly shut the door behind me and walked down to the lobby with a spring in my step.

"I wonder what goodies await me! Oh, boy!" I danced a little.

Spotlights illuminated the raindrops outside as they fell. I shielded my eyes from their luminescence. The scurrying of feet rustled across the asphalt and concrete like ants trying to take a god! I dared not stand still, ants could still ruin your picnic basket. Bullets pelted the doorway as I dove to safety preemptively.

I bounced around in the cover of the night, taking soldiers down with grace and cunning. The first fell behind a police cruiser, completely unaware of my presence. The next was taken beside his comrades, they were never the wiser, and soon I took care of them. After a while, I lost track of how many were stricken down by my wrath. It was boring to fight weaklings, a ninja needs to constantly sharpen his skills, less they dull.

It was clear once a few remained that my entertainment was concluding. I thirsted for a challenge and the universe answered my wish with... that girl again... WHAT!? Bad universe! The girl had suited back up and returned for seconds. Now, I appreciated a girl with a healthy appetite, but she was no match for me.

"This time I'm going to kick your fat ass!" she declared.

I scoffed at the idea, "You should try to graduate from your training bra first before you try to take me, little lady."

"You are such an asshole!"

"Excuse me!" I snapped with an offended tone, "I am a man of intellect. I do not sully the purity of knowledge with baseless, unfounded opinions. I deal in FACTS!" I said, sticking my tongue out.

She seemed very determined to change facts, but the poor girl just didn't understand. I wasn't ready to implement the final phase of my plan, I had time to play with her. We charged across the roof, fighting from behind the spotlights. It was personal for her, women always make things personal, it was a shame really. Nevertheless, she had her rifle slipped on her back, she was set on fighting with her combat knife.

I would grant her as much with my athema, a fight I had easily won before. Her strikes were faster, wilder, her emotions clouded her judgment. Letting their emotions get the better of them, when will they learn? Admittedly, her increased speed made it easier to find an opening. One need only wait and it would present itself.

However, she pinched my blade between her knee and elbow. She not only stopped my strike but kept me from going on the defensive. Her next slashes came with precision as she planned her attacks, I'd been tricked. I evaded, but she would not release my blade. Eventually, she lost balance, but instead of falling, she twisted and tossed my blade across the roof.

"NOOOO, not my athema!" I screamed as I ran after it.

It skidded to a stop at the edge of the rain-slick roof. I scurried to it with great joy in my heart as I grasped it. She snuck up behind me and kicked my magnificent butt. I flipped over the edge, flailing my arms for something to grab. Luckily, a small service ladder saved me from the alley below.

I hurried down in a panicked, and halfway the ladder broke from the wall. I had failed to notice it was rusted to the bone. The lower half tipped back, and it came crashing down on me as I hit the ground. With the ladder broken, there was no way she could follow.

I rolled it off of me and stumbled to my feet. Not that a girl had hurt me or anything, I was just winded from all the exercise, a desk job does that to you. I waddled down the alley and turned around to taunt her. My eyes leaped forth when I saw her drop two floors onto a dumpster. She rolled off it and ran at me like a cheetah.

I found myself before the hotel with her hot on my trail. I ducked behind a police cruiser near the trunk and waited.

"You're not going to win this!" I shouted with bravado.

In turn, snickers echoed through the silent night. It was quiet, the raindrops splashing were louder than my heartbeats.

"What's so funny, girly?" I asked, "You think you can beat someone of my intellect. I'm better and you know it. Give up while you can."

There was no response, she had gone strangely silent. How could she suppress her presence so skillfully? A noise came across from the hotel, was it her? Another noise shot out loudly, and I moved to the next car. A spinning trash can lid startled me, had she circled around that quickly?

"You're pretty good for a girl, I'll admit it." I shouted, "I am a man, a skilled warrior, like a ninja speeding through the darkness, and I will swiftly end you. You will never stop the hurricane of badass I have become from my years of hardship and training. Let's end this, I have things to do!"

"My thoughts exactly!" she whispered into my ear.

I spun around as fast as I could and got kicked in the balls. I fell, holding my bruised ego and she smiled. She drew her sidearm and put one in my chest. Her face twisted with satisfaction as the bullet pierced and blood splattered out on the rain-soaked streets.

She stood over me with a smug grin, "What was that!? How's it feel to get your ass beat by a woman, you sexist pig!?"

"Bu-But, I'm too young and beautiful to die... Master, are you proud of me?" I gasped with my last breath of air and died...

CHAPTER 14
THIS ISN'T MY BANK AFTER ALL

FAIRWATER, THE NEXT DAY, AUGUST 28TH – The White Tiger was haunted by the echoes of a dark voice as he napped on the bank's doorstep.

A dark chill went down my spine as if someone horrible had called out to me. My peaceful sleep was broken, and I awoke with a yawn and stretched before I realized I had slept a day away. The bank was open, it worked out anyway. I slid my hands into my pockets and went inside. I quickly pulled out my book, so I wouldn't have to talk to anyone.

It also provided the chance to continue my reading while I waited in line. The bank may have sucked, but not as much as the ones that sucked so much that I could not allow them to survive. Sinister intent implied. My eyes wandered as I read, I sized up the building, identified the genera of the plants, and counted the people, fatties were worth two! However, I couldn't shake this uneasy feeling, there was a foul odor on the air.

Not too long after, the doors burst open, and five armed men rushed into the bank. They executed their entrance horribly, completely disorganized. From henceforth I would refer to them as Thug A through E, I couldn't be bothered to remember unimportant people. One fired his gun, a real lackluster fellow trying to establish dominance as the leader.

He screamed, "Everybody down! If you do as I say, only a few of you might get shot! Hahahaha!" he laughed, but his humor must have been an acquired taste.

They were thugs without masks and cocky, they wanted people to know who they were. I recognized their tattoos as one of the local gangs, the Black Suns. A group of thugs that pulled muscle heads off the streets and put guns in their hands. I wasn't impressed, I didn't even care, but it was another hassle the universe had thrown at me. Everyone dove to the floor as they screamed, while I calmly closed my book, and proceeded to beat myself over the head with it.

"Come on, can't I get a break, please!?" I begged aloud, "I've been a good boy, and I'm not talking to you Santa... You know who you are!" I pointed up, "And also, my poor, innocent book is damaged thanks to you."

Being the only one not on the floor, Thug A, also known as the so-called leader put his shotgun in my face, "Get on the ground, or I'll rearrange your face!"

I casually slid my book back into my jacket and said, "What, that floor!?" while pointing down, "You do mean the floor, right, cause that's floor? The ground has dirt, but I can see your confusion. The floor is dirty, so I'll let it pass."

He tried to pull the trigger, but I moved the barrel to the side and caused him to lose his grip. The gun slipped and he fumbled it into my hands. I smacked his face with the butt of the gun and he stumbled back. I released the gun and dropped it as bait. Thug A wasn't even close to getting it back as I caught it by the barrel with my foot, like balancing a broom.

I tilted the gun forward and he slammed his face into the butt of the gun. Tenacity was Thug A's forte, he quickly recovered and attacked. I tripped him with my foot, bashed him on the back of the head with the gun, and knocked him out. It had been a hassle, and I would have rather not dealt with it in the first place. Nevertheless, I unloaded the gun, stripping it down in one fluid motion, then threw the pieces to the floor before stepping over Thug A's body.

"I realized I don't need money after all." I told them as I walked away with my hands in my pockets, "I'll get out of your way..."

"You took down, "????", you're not getting out of here alive!" the biggest guy screamed.

I could have sworn he said Thug A's real name, but I couldn't be bothered to remember.

He pulled out a pistol as I turned around to leave and fired. I felt the air shift and spun around as I drew my sword, slicing the bullet in two before sheathing my blade. The bullet split down the middle and the two pieces went around me. I had done it so fast, I doubted anyone seen how awesome I was.

"Wow, you have really bad aim!" I smirked, taunting them but everyone muttered Sleeper, and the room flooded with panic, "Hey, the only thing super about me is my good looks! Don't blame me for his bad aim and you..." I said, looking at the big guy, "If you insist on fighting me, I won't hold back." I said as I gripped my katana, "I'll give you two options, option A, you leave, option B... Well, it's more of an or else really."

Most of their bullets were half aimed and were easy enough the evade. The ones that didn't miss I dealt with personally. The first one came at my head, I sliced it, and they took down Thugs D and E or was it C and D? Their wounds were nothing fatal, but they couldn't fight anymore.

I smirked, "Wow, I know you had a split decision on your hands, but shooting your allies, isn't that a bit low for even crooks?"

"How are you doing that!?" and "He has to be a Sleeper, right!?" were the hot questions.

The two remaining thugs were impressed, "We could use a Sleeper like you. Our boss, Cutter, is always looking for fresh meat!"

"I'm sorry..." I said, "I can't hear what you're saying over the crap coming out of your mouth."

"How dare you!"

"I have no interest in joining a pathetic gang, especially, a small one!"

"I'll teach you to fuck with the Black Suns!"

Thug Q poked his head around his cover to shoot, but I had already snuck behind him. I dispatched him with a kick to the head. Thug Red spotted me, but I grabbed a stapler from the counter and threw it. It smacked him in the face, and he was down for the count.

I hastily made my way out with a sigh, "It is such a burden to be awesome."

Fate, as it would seem, had a different plan in mind as I found two more thugs outside. My guess, they were the driver and more backup, just my luck. I tried to be good and keep my head down so I didn't get hassled, so bothersome. I moved quickly and stood between them without notice.

"Hello." I casually said as I waved with a smile which startled them.

They drew their guns, but they were too slow. I knocked the firearms from their hands simultaneously. I twisted one of the thug's arms and left him open to break his arm with my knee. Their actions were easy to read and too sluggish to be a threat. I spun around to stop the other thug's attack and kicked him in the leg.

I felt the bone break and he dropped to the ground. With my foot, I struck the last standing thug's weak points.

He fell, and I grabbed them both by an arm. I twisted them straight and pinned them down. The tension in their arms could be felt in my fingers as I applied pressure.

I heard a subtle, almost click like sound as their shoulders popped out of their sockets. The pain itself had almost knocked them out, but I grabbed them by their hair. I bashed their heads together and knocked them unconscious. It was already my intention to leave, but the sirens reminded me I needed to put some spring in my step. The police were slow in response, and I was long gone before they showed up.

Fate, was a heartless bitch, for I thought I was safe, yet again, I was in more danger. An evil sensation ran down my spine, I could feel the corruption carried on the wind. I turned my head, and I saw the source of the vile feeling running at me with hundreds of arms and legs.

It was a horde of something most unholy, "Ah..." I said in disgust, "Fangirls..."

Their numbers were uncountable, and their ages varied widely, from teens all the way to late thirties.

The front lines screamed in unison, "There he is girls, get him!"

"Strange, it's not even Thursday yet.

My stomach turned inside out, and I ran as fast as I could. I ducked into the first hiding spot I could find, and they ran past. I waited until I was sure the coast was clear.

"It is to be expected, I am awesome." I said with a frown, "Fangirls are dedicated, but luckily for me, they're not too bright… and also have short life expectancies. Haven't quite figured that one out yet."

My voice reverberated against the walls and echoed back as, "You suck!"

"I see, hello, Eleven. If you make me frown anymore, my face will get stuck like this. Then think how upset those lunatics would be."

I turned to see Eleven walk from the shadows in his grey pinstripe suit.

"I'd say it was nice to see you Shaw, but I think you're an ass." he said with dissatisfaction, "Then again, I hate everyone."

"I don't care."

Eleven expressed a quizzical look, "Not even a little curious how I got here?"

"The gateways were clearly fixed. It's not difficult to figure out."

"Actually, we need to talk. Walk with me." I sighed but reluctantly followed, "All the gateways were destroyed by the criminal Zero Heal when he escaped his execution as you know. He successfully prevented us from following him and then some. We've spent all our time and resources restoring just the one gateway. The criminal's execution is of the highest priority, the higher-ups want blood for the murder of the high priestess.

We only got the gateway working a week ago, and we've been playing catch-up ever since. The world has changed a lot over the past six months..."

"Get to the point!" I interrupted, "I'm the only agent in the ONA familiar with this area, and you've got a job they want me to do."

"Right to the point." he huffed, "Our researchers have been investigating the high priestess's files. For some time now we have known she was looking into a book. Her notes aren't specific, but she believed it to be of great evil. Her investigation says this book moves around, never in one place too long.

However, with the Hellgate, they can't get the book out of this city. We have had a scout in place looking for the book. We have received a report it's been found, and we want you to meet the scout. There is a possible connection between this book and Zero Heal." he pulled a piece of folded paper from his pocket, "Here is the location." and we stopped in front of a cafe as he passed me the paper.

"I love doing grunt work. That is literally my favorite thing, ever." I said as I took the paper.

An urgent news report was broadcast on the TV in the cafe. We stepped in to watch...

"Yesterday night, we lost contact with Clearcrest. The SAS scouting jet reported our worst fears. Upon arrival, the Crystal Haven Hellgate and the entire city were both found destroyed. It is unclear at this point how many lives have been lost, but the city's airships were missing. It is assumed there are survivors. The SAS has begun an extensive search for them!"

The cafe was sent into a panic and made it impossible to hear each other. We stepped back outside.

Under my breath, I said, "One down, nineteen to go. How much longer can humanity hold out against the darkness that lurks outside the Hellgates, I wonder?"

Eleven sighed, "It's almost been a year since the Event, and now, people live inside these Hellgates waiting for the day they fall and they're eaten alive."

I continued with my train of thought, "Or will humanity pull off a miracle and draw some light out of the darkness, saving itself. I don't think we can when we still fall for things like avarice and vanity. We were a doomed race to begin with, I think even our gods lost faith."

I looked at the sky shrouded in a vast sea of grey, sorrowful clouds that flowed by, "Even the sky has forsaken us and has stolen the sun from our sight. The sky has hidden behind this cloak of misfortune for over six months. The Earth weeps over the pain the disease that is man has wrought. It's sorrow taking the sky, making the sun like our hope, a fleeting memory."

Eleven grew bored, "Listen, this has been fun, and by fun, I mean boring, and by this, I mean you." he said, "I wish something interesting would happen. Until then, I'm out of here." and he walked away.

I figured I'd get started on the mission and headed out to the point of contact. On my way, a deep breeze chilled me to the bone.

I shivered, "These winds are strange tides to even me now. Maybe they'll carry that change you were wishing for, but there is a foul odor on them too. Who knows what will become of us in the end. Maybe nothing will change, or maybe we won't even recognize ourselves tomorrow..."

CHAPTER 15
FOLLOWING THE TRAIL

CLEARCREST, THE NIGHT BEFORE, THE 27TH -- Little Red continued to look for clues in the cold, wet air.

I could only hear the sounds of water. The rain pelted my umbrella, and my shoes splashed puddles. It was dark, all the easier to see her soul drifting aimlessly. She seemed almost lost, moving around and pausing. It was like she was scratching her head as she tried to recall a memory.

None of the tombstones or statues had any importance, maybe she was looking for landmarks. It took forever to navigate the graveyard, it was a maze. Strangely, I was sure it was smaller, it had taken me less than an hour before. She must have been lost, it was dark enough to lose your way. Eventually, we found the streets.

My head was filled with fuzzy images of buildings, streetlights, and neon signs. Everything was jumbled, disorganized, and out of place. Her thoughts were screwing with the way I saw the world. Then, like magic, I was standing in front of a building with her soul bouncing off the front door. You can never be too careful, so I took a look around outside.

Behind the bar was a small pathway closed off with a chain link fence behind a wooden one. The wood was busted up, and the chain-link had been cut and swung like a shower curtain. With nothing out of the ordinary, I decided to go in. I walked up to the front door which was pretty solid. Her soul bounced off the door because she wasn't invited.

Every area had its own field, and for some reason, ghosts can't enter freely. I wasn't too sure, it could have been nonsense. I had to open the door for her, and she floated in. As I squeezed past people, I went unnoticed me. Her soul went to the bar and hovered over the counter.

It felt as if she was waiting for something, and I sat. Next to me was a big guy with his arms covered in tattoos.

I normally didn't talk to others but felt compelled, "You've got nice tattoos. I especially like the skulls and busty chicks."

He moved his bottle almost to his lips before stopping and looked at me.

He grunted, like a simple acknowledgment. He went back to his drink and it got awkward. I went back to waiting silently, but it was boring. As I waited, my eyes slowly drifted to the TV hanging behind the bar.

"Welcome to another episode of The Brilliant and Famous! Tonight we take a closer look at the life of the world-renowned, Andrew Inferious. The sole man whose intelligence kept America from falling back to the middle ages after the Revelation Outbreak. His scientific genius helped restore this country, giving us back electricity, fresh water, and creating powerful electric engines. These breakthroughs have helped us live more comfortably and have given the government vehicles to combat the Sleepers.

It's thanks to him that society hasn't crumbled, and we can start to recover as a people. His mind is without a doubt the greatest in our time, quite possibly ever. Later in an interview, he'll talk more about his ideas into replenishing food sources, he's even hinted that he's already working on something. Until then, let's take a closer look at his beginnings, and like most, they began humbly..."

He seemed like he was the exact kind of man who would be up on capitol hill. My trance with the TV broke when her soul whipped past me. She swirled around a man who walked in from the back. He was the bartender, was I supposed to talk to him? I motioned him over, and he gestured back.

I turned back to the big guy next to me, "You know, I've got a tattoo of my own as well."

He turned to me again, his expression looked mad, but I think his face just looked that way.

"Yeah, it's a pretty black kitty cat, right here." I told him as I pulled my skirt back and showed him my inner thigh.

When I looked down, there wasn't one, but there should have been a black cat, "Well, I guess that's where I want to get one. I was so excited about it, I forgot I hadn't gotten it yet..." I said as I knocked my head with my tongue sticking out.

I lowered my skirt back down and turned away from him. I couldn't understand, I swore I had one. That's when the bartender caught my attention.

"What can I get you?" he asked.

I was shy and hesitant, "Umm... I... I need to ask you something. Th-There was a girl in here a week ago, she was a frequent visitor. I wanted to know if..."

His face twisted with anger, "You're here about the girl who was murdered, just like the others!"

"N-No, I just want to know about... the woman with her..."

"I know exactly what you're here for!" he said sharply, "You're one of those hunters that get themselves killed and those around them trying to win the glory of killing Sleepers!" and he leaned over into my face, "I don't like Sleepers, but I don't like your kind even more little girl. You look like you're barely out of a training bra! Go home before you get someone killed! Now, get out!" and he stormed off.

I was offended, "I'm 19..." but he was gone.

"Don't worry about him, he's got a stick up his ass." I thought that my ears were deceiving me, and I turned to my right, "You've got nice tits too!" sure enough, the big guy was finally speaking.

"See..." I said using my finger to motion back and forth between the two of us, "This is nice. This is us bonding! And you're just saying that!" and I waved with a smile.

"I call'em as I see'em." he said before taking a sip of his beer.

He was nice and was very accommodating when I asked to get a picture with him. I half smiled, and he tipped his bottle, giving cheers. A good photo, but I should have smiled.

As I put my phone away, someone got close behind me, "Meet me out back, I might know something that could help." and she walked away shouting at the bartender, "Jess, I'm taking a break!"

She was a waitress, and the bartender yelled back, "Don't take long like you usually do, you hear me!? Five minutes! I'm not in the mood tonight."

She went out the backdoor near the bathrooms at the edge of the room, and the soul floated after her. My guess was she could be trusted or knew something useful. Jess would get suspicious if I followed her out, but I remembered the broken fence. I left out the front and snuck around the side. Squeezing through was easy, but there was nobody waiting for me.

I heard the sound of water, but it had stopped raining. I saw steam rise from behind a dumpster, and put it together. If you gotta go, you gotta go, but now, I did too. I began to squirm in my skirt.

"Sorry!" she said, rising and zipping her pants, "The guys in there don't respect the boundaries of the women's bathroom." she rolled her eyes as she stepped out, "If you want privacy, you have to resort to the dumpster." and she leaned against the brick wall next to us, "So, what's the name, blondie?"

"Call me, Red." I wasn't a trusting person, "You said you might be able to help me?"

"Are you really one of those hunters!?" she said with a smile, ignoring my question.

"I'm just looking for someone..." and she cut me off.

"That's cool!" she said with crossed arms, "I've always thought fighting those things was cool, but I couldn't do it. You must be tough for a small lady!" she said, sizing me up, "I'm sorry for the way he acted, his daughter was killed because of a hunter. He was stupid, and she got caught in the crossfire.

The hunter ended up killing her when he blew the Sleeper up. So, Jess doesn't like hunters, calls them monsters just the same. Cut him some slack, even if he's always had the stick up his ass."

God, this girl loved to talk, I had to speed things along, "Will you help me?"

She stepped away from the wall, "You didn't hear this from me, but that girl came in here all the time. Her name was Jennifer, and she was usually in here with a friend. The two of them were always hitting the bars to find guys to rub up on. What girl doesn't these days, not a lot to hold you back since the world went to shit, right? The two were always together without fail, but for some reason, Jennifer was alone that night.

I saw her leave with this girl in purple. I didn't see Jennifer as a muff diver, but this girl was admittedly hot!" and she paused for a moment, "You didn't hear that!" and gestured by zipping her lips, "Now, the two grinded on one another for a while before leaving. I had never seen the girl in purple before, and I can't remember what she looked like. They were awfully familiar if you know what I mean, maybe the friend might know something.

If I've learned one thing about killers, Sleeper or not, they stalk their prey. Maybe the friend knows something. Her name's Virginia, and she works a couple blocks that way at the "Crimson Flames" strip club." she said as she turned back to the bar, "Oh, the name's Amanda, I've got to get back to work before Jess has an aneurysm. Try not to get killed, Red!" she gave me a thumbs up and was gone.

I may not have gotten much, but a lead meant it wasn't a dead end. I began making my way in the direction Amanda had pointed. It was nice to be back on the streets, it was peaceful as I passed several blocks of derelict buildings following the girl's soul. Littering the streets were homeless by the hundreds everywhere I looked. Dangerous wasn't a strong enough word to describe the situation there.

It was cold, they huddled around fires to keep warm, those who couldn't, froze. The harsher the conditions, the more desperate the people would get. I had to keep my head down and keep out of sight. Normally, I would have blended in, but something was off. The people around me had taken to wearing these weird porcelain rabbit masks, horror movie creepy.

When people dress uniformly like some kind of cult, things get… weird. I avoided them and kept my head down as I followed her soul. Finding the doorstep of the strip club got me out of the lion's den. The door blocked her like last time, and I wasted no time getting out of the cold. The warmth melted the chill that clung to my skin.

Fog cascaded across the floor, and multicolored lights flashed into the foyer. Something felt weird about the place, but her soul led me farther in. Around the corner, I found myself inside a large open room. It was packed to the brim with people and beautiful dancers on stage. Most of what I saw, I didn't know the human body could do.

They were all very pretty, the men and women alike on stage. They were a little distracting, but that was the point, right? I didn't like their clothes but those wouldn't last long anyway. The heels would definitely get my neck broken. Enjoying the show wouldn't get me anywhere, and I got back to looking around.

I noticed the girl's soul buzzing in circles, I assumed it was to get my attention. The people were huddled near the stage, making it easy to move around. After a while, I noticed some of the masked nuts had followed me in. Who knew if anything would happen, but never trust anyone who hides their face. The way they were spread out made it tedious to avoid them.

I found her soul in front of a bulletin board. She swirled near some pictures, and I examined them. A picture labeled Virginia popped out, giving me a face to work with. The picture was of poor quality, it was useless to me. Instead, I looked at the dancers on stage hoping to spot her.

A shiver chilled my spine as more masked freaks showed up. You couldn't turn without bumping into one. She wasn't on stage, and I wanted to get away from the nutbags. She could have been off work, the fastest way to find out was to ask someone.

I spotted the bouncer down in the dumps at the bar and approached him, "Umm, sorry for bothering you, but is Virginia working tonight?" he was a small guy.

"What's it to you?" he asked.

"I need to ask her a few questions." I explained, "I'm looking for a friend, and someone said Virginia would be able to help me." I said, playing it cool.

He looked at me for a moment, "I'll see if she wants to talk to you." and he went backstage.

I waited at the bar, focusing on the flashing lights, music, and the dancers. Eventually, he came back with a worried look on his face.

He paused, trying to collect his words, "She was supposed to be here hours ago, but no one's seen her." he was very distressed, "Virginia's a straight arrow, mostly, and a hard worker. She's never late, never, and in a town like this, that definitely means something bad."

Bad things happen, more so now than ever, but what were the odds?

"Do you know where she lives?" I asked, "I could check on her at the same time..."

"No... I don't know where any of the girls live."

Maybe it wasn't a complete loss, had to stay positive "Do you have a picture of her?"

"Yeah!" he said, jumping behind the bar, "The girls like to party, and God do they love to take their pictures of themselves." he told me as he grabbed a photo frame from the wall and showed me, "This one here is her." he pointed.

It was a good one, and I snapped a shot of it with my phone, "Thanks! Do you know what direction she leaves in?"

"She always goes to the right after her shift. Beyond that, I don't know. I'm sorry I can't help more."

"No." I smiled with a thumbs up, "You've been more than helpful! Somebody has to have seen her." and he smiled.

It was time to begin the hunt again, even for a small chance someone knew her. However, hopeless came to mind as the word to describe my efforts, as no one had. Most ran when I spoke to them, trust was hard to come by. My search led me to a large crowd of people. They always feel safer in groups, someone was bound to be more talkative. They were so loud, I couldn't hear myself speak.

Everyone seemed interested with something else, they were definitely distracted.

It all blurred together, "Did you see it?", "What the hell could do that?", "It's horrible.", "Poor girl...", "It had to be a Sleeper, right?", "They'll kill us all!","Sleepers are evil!", "Sleeper!", "I didn't know a person had so much blood.", "So many pieces, was she bitten or ripped apart?"

No, it couldn't have been, she was my only lead! I pushed my way through to the center of the crowd. I stumbled forward and saw a car with the backdoor open and blood everywhere. Bumping against people along the way, I moved closer. A woman, covered in blood was missing her midsection and her legs were on the ground.

Her face was impossible to make out from so far away. I moved closer and saw it was Virginia. The blood was fresh, she couldn't have been dead long. There was no way she was killed by chance, I was followed. She was a message meant for me, she was here, and she was watching.

What else could it have been? What were the odds of finding the woman I was looking for, killed by the murderer I was hunting, the day I got in the city!? Her body was clearly left out in the open for me. I wanted to examine the body for clues, but the police were coming. I'd never see the body once they took it away.

Before anything could be done, I realized I'd been surrounded by the masked weirdos, now dressed in white coats. They all mumbled, chanting incoherently like some prayer. They reached out toward me, and I tripped into more trying to escape. Their hands were wrapping around me like a straight jacket. I fought until I had freed myself.

There was nothing that would stop me from running, they'd never catch me...

DarkSide Chronicles: 1

Suddenly, I awoke from my long slumber and saw the night sky. I saw a strange new land, different, but not so unlike the one I had grown accustomed to. How long had I been asleep for the disgusting humans to have created so much? No, more importantly, something dark had awoken me, and I saw this man dressed in a black hooded coat before me, sitting on the edge of the building kicking his feet. Silently, he watched from above as a girl in red screamed.

A woman stepped from the shadows, barely revealing her form. A transparent purple cloak hung as low as her short purple skirt, she was dressed like a concubine. She ran her fingers under her skirt, rubbing her body as she licked the blood from her fingers.

"Umm..." she moaned, "That was tasty. It feels sooooo good to be full."

The man in black spoke, "The game is about to begin. We haven't even moved our first piece," he was upset, "and here you are doing things on your own!"

"But she's so fun to play with!" she said excitedly.

"She's the first piece." his feet idled as he looked back, "You're not to break the rules of the game again. Nothing goes according to plan, but you will not act on your own. Do it again and I'll kill you both."

"I was having a little fun." she said with attitude as she stomped her heel, "Don't get your dick bent."

He snapped, "Leave before I kill you!" he snapped his fingers and darkness rose behind them without form.

She rolled her eyes, "Fine..."

When the darkness faded, she was gone, and he continued to watch from above with a smile on his face. This man, there was something about him, something very dark. For once, in a long time, I was excited about something in this hell hole. I couldn't help but wonder what he had planned, it might be interesting. This new world left me to wonder the possibilities...

CHAPTER 16
THE HIGH SEAS

FAIRWATER, THE 27TH -- The Silver Bullet had a plan, and you can bet there's a method to his madness, probably... maybe... I don't know...

Sometime after my usual morning routine at any given local pub, I thought I'd earn some funds the honest way for the day's round of drinks. I set up shop, I knew a guy and got a booth for cheap. I've had some sales experience in the past, and I was pretty good at it.

I knew exactly how to pitch my product to the masses, "Get your fish, I've got fresh fish! Get your fish." I smiled a little, "Damn I'm good."

From the corner of my eyes, I saw two coppers walking closer. Pigs can't handle my sizzle. THE MAN WILL NOT KEEP ME DOWN! It wasn't long before they stepped forward.

Officer Bourne leaned against my booth, "What have we told you?"

I brushed my hair to the side, I had this, "Officers..." I was as cool as ice, "THIS ISN'T MY BOOTH!" I yelled, sweating buckets, "It's a friend's, yeah, a friend's... Want some fish?" I said, holding up a piece, "You can't have my fish!" and I smacked him, "You see, my friend stepped away, and I'm watching it for him..." and they weren't buying it, plan B, "Tell'em, Ralph!"

Ralph slowly raised above the counter, "Hello, fine gents! What he says is true."

I smiled, "See, it's not my booth, I'm just looking after it for a friend... What's with all these questions!?" I said, panicking, "I didn't sleep with your wife! I'M NOT TELLING YOU MY NAME!!!"

Ralph screamed, "Shut up, Ron, you're gonna blow it." as he hit me in the side.

"You sold me out, you traitor!" I said, poking him in the eyes.

Officer Menendez broke us up, "Ron, it doesn't matter whether or not it's your booth. It's perfectly legal to have a booth, but what's not is you having it parked smack dab in the middle of an intersection. You're holding up traffic."

I looked around, and sure enough, I was sitting in a four-way intersection, "Had not noticed this... awkward!" then I smiled, "Awkward for YOU that is!" I said, holding up a piece of paper, "I have a permit to sell my good in the middle of this intersection between the hours of two and four, signed by the mayor himself. Isn't that right Ralph?"

"Yep, yep!" he said.

"Okay, Ron..." Officer Bourne said, "Say we didn't believe you, for argument's sake. Let me point out several holes in your story. One, your permit is in crayon and looks like a two-year-old drew it. Two, we don't have a mayor, not since before the Revelation Outbreak. Three, we've had this exact conversation before."

"Nu-uh!" I said, "Ralph wasn't here the last three times."

Officer Menendez said, "You're very bad at ventriloquism, I can see your mouth moving, and a sock puppet does not make a good alibi."

I shook my head, "No, no, you've got it all wrong. I have a condition that makes the corner of my mouth move whenever I hear puppets talk."

"Puppets don't talk, people do." Officer Bourne said.

"I know, weird, right!? But it happens, ain't that right, Ralph!?" I nodded.

"Fuck you, Ron!" Ralph rudely screamed.

I'd had enough of Ralph's nonsense, "Fuck me? Fuck ME!? Fuck YOU!"

"You've already got your hand up my ass, there isn't much more you could!" the smartass said.

An evil glare came over my face, it must have looked pretty weird, "Oh, you like that, don't you, you sicko." and I gasped, "WAIT, I have an idea!" and I pointed dramatically behind the two officers, "Look over there!" and I ran.

I ran and ran until my legs were about to give out. Running is hard when you've got the fuzz on you, but a man's gotta do what a man's gotta do. Life on the run wasn't easy, there were times I thought I'd never make it. It felt like forever, but when I thought they'd finally forgotten about me, I headed back. Only, when I had returned, I found nothing more than a run-down shack.

"Oh, the humanity!" I screamed as I beat the ground with my fist. "Crap, you're still here!?" I said in shock as the two cops looked at me.

"You ran out one end of the booth and into the other end, where you suddenly began beating the ground for no reason."

"That was a bad idea..." I said, catching my breath.

Ralph rolled his eyes, "What part of that idea sounded smart to you. Next time, let's keep the pants on, shall we?"

My rage hit the boiling point, "I've got another idea!"

I reached out, grabbed both of the officers' noses and pulled down hard, before poking them in the eyes. I ran for the hills like a madman, flailing my arms in the air. I hid in an alleyway and looked to see if we were followed.

Ralph slowly poked his head out and screamed, "He's back here!"

"You damn, traitor!" I shouted, "This friendship is over, you're dead to me."

A couple of shotgun blasts left Ralph choking on his own blood as I walked away.

His final words were, "Oh, come on... can't you take a joke!?"

Finally, free of that nuisance once and for all put pep back in my step, until I saw it. The source of all evil, an evil that had haunted humanity since... well, for a really long time. The structure sat there watching, judging, and plotting as I saw its sinister aura corrupt the sky above. The sky grew dark beyond it, and lightning split the backdrop. A seriousness like this hadn't come over me in a long time.

I pointed out, screaming to let it know I wasn't standing for its wicked ways.

"Stop mocking me!" then the bells of the church rang, and I took off like a frightened schoolgirl with my tail between my legs and my arms flailing again.

It was time, I had to prepare. I gathered arms for the upcoming war, ran the streets naked, and even talked to a twenty-foot tall shadow lady. With preparations made, I gathered my crew for one last job, and we set out on the open seas. I had always felt at ease on the waves, I guess it really was a pirate's life for me. We battled many ships for the right of passage, for pirates follow nothing but gold, women, and mead. We fought the red-headed serpent that halted our voyage.

We duked it out with the wizard of the sky, shattering his red power. Striking as he drew in yellow lightning, and stole from him his green aura to light the way on dark nights. We sailed the black tar pits of the black sea and paddled the stony waters. Soon, in our sights was our goal, and we would not back down, not after coming this far. However, before us stood an invisible barrier in the middle of the ocean, barring passage.

With all our might we shattered it to find a strange new sea of cloth. It was unlike anything I had ever seen, but on the horizon, we saw the promised land. Slowly, we persevered, reduced to a crawl as we traversed the estuary of this forbidden land. Finally, we made it to the land of dreams. We could see the beautiful women, bouncing breasts, curvy bodies, perfect butts, and legs that went for miles.

It had taken an eternity to find this paradise, and many men were lost. Only I and six of my most trusted crew had survived this arduous journey. Down to a simple rowboat, but we had found our treasure.

We shouted in unison with a great cheer, "Row, row, row your boat, gently down the stream!"

The women waved to us from secluded islands that displayed them like trophies. We would not stand for such treatment of women.

"Aye, men! We rescue them all, not a single one left behind!" I proclaimed victoriously.

What kind of man would leave beautiful women to the unforgiving sea?

I spotted more in the distance, "Hold steady, you scalawags, there be more off yonder. I will return with their precious booties."

I leaped from the boat, heroically donning my authentic Viking attire.

My crew screamed out, "No Captain, ye be wearing heavy armor. Ye can't swim like that!"

I had not realized it, but they were right. With the knowledge, I fell to my knees and flopped like a fish out of water. My loyal crew wasted no time coming to my aid and jumped to the edge of the boat. They extended their hands to their limits, but it was no good. It was too late for me, I was at the mercy of the sea.

My first mate, however, would not stand for this tragic end and cleaved the armor from his flesh. He dove in with no hesitation and backflipped as I clapped in amazement. He landed on his feet perfectly, a ten out of ten in my book, and he ran to my side. Throwing my arm over his shoulder, he carried me back to the boat. Caring not for his own safety, he threw me in first and followed second.

I sat up like nothing had happened, "You are a first-class hero, my good sir, and it WILL..." I said, pointing up dramatically, "be reflected in your share of the booty."

The crew cheered for my quick recovery and began rowing with me at the head of the ship once more. In the far distance, I saw a stone giant standing speechless with a blank gaze. We saved as many women as we could and sailed from the promised land. Before we could leave, the stone giant sprang to life, drawing a weapon equal in size and swung at us with great force. We had no time to escape, we were left to whatever fate the gods would force upon us.

NO, I would not be controlled by gods, and I charged the beast, and ahh! She wouldn't stop hitting me over the head with a broom, screaming some nonsense about getting out of the store. I ripped the broom from her hands and held it above my head, screaming in victory as we sailed back into the open seas with what we had looted from the adult video store...

CHAPTER 17
THE WOMAN AND THE ARMORED CAR

F41RW4T3R, T1M3 UNK0WN -- The Shadow Diva reveled, conning bitches was her second favorite pastime.

My smile reached from ear to ear, I could have skipped down the street. As if, but I was pleased with all the shiny new things I had "acquired". I tossed the bag of jewels up and down, thinking of everything I could buy. All the things I could do with it, like what to sell and keep. I could melt down the useless things like the candlesticks.

Not that I had anyone who could do that anymore, "The fucking asshole!"

Before I had a chance to spiral down that dark hole, I was interrupted by screams as a swarm of people ran past me. There was something ahead of me, sending the people into a panic. I didn't care what it was, even if it was the most wanted man in the world, I wasn't going to go over there... Though, if there was some kind of accident, there was only one thing for a beautiful woman like myself to do...

"There could be a reward for any beautiful heroines that "saved" the day." I thought.

I found a dark place to hide my goodies and ran toward the panic. The hardest part was fighting against the flow, but it thinned out fast. There weren't many cars, but there were a few. I could have picked locks, but I said fuck it and started bashing windows. There was shit to find, but what would I have expected the average Joe to have.

Every now and again, someone would run by, and I acted the part and waved. Look like you belong, and a pretty smile never hurt. It didn't take long to find all the cars were empty. There was nothing I hated more than getting all excited with no payoff. Out of nowhere, I saw the holy grail, the accident that sent the people running.

Around the corner was an armored truck flipped on its side, "Sweet!" I said enthusiastically, "Unprotected valuables just ripe for the picking!"

Right there in front of me was the biggest payday I'd seen in a long time. Best part, it was the truck from the Cardigan building. I felt it was my civic duty to use this karmic twist to rob the bitch blind... again! No one and I mean no one gets a look at the lady goods... not without a shiny down payment first. I made a mad dash for the overturned truck, but I stopped halfway.

There was black smoke rising from it. If it was a snake, I'd have been bitten. How had I not noticed it before? The smoke, the truck on its side, there had been an attack, and they better not have taken all the loot! I ran up to it and looked around to see if anyone important was taking notice. I was sure everyone was more worried about their own asses.

Using the underside of the truck, I was able to get to the top. When I got to there, I found myself staring at a massive hole. It was a perfect circle, clearly, a bomb hadn't done it, but the metal told me a story. It was caused by heat, lacked fractures in the metal, and it was rough like sandpaper. The explosion had come from the outside, had to be a Sleeper.

That meant whatever was in this truck was definitely worth stealing! I was about to jump in when I heard chains rattle inside. I had gotten ahead of myself and didn't stop to think that the someone who had done this might still be inside. In my haste, I had gotten careless, and I held off. My senses told me there was only one person, but I could barely see past the smoke.

They weren't moving, and I saw a web of chains lining the inside. All of them converged on the figure in the center of the truck. That's when I realized they WERE the loot, it was a prisoner. That changed everything... there wasn't decent cash in selling slaves. Didn't matter, I didn't do slavery, more people just complicated deals.

If I had known that from the beginning, I wouldn't have wasted my time. I was about to turn away when a shiver went down my spine. The smoke had gone thin for a moment and I recognized the prisoner. She was the one with the bag on her head from the Cardigan building.

"Who was she, and how was she important to that bitch!?" I asked.

As the smoke cleared, I could see fragments of the metal scattered throughout. Around her neck, a steel collar, and from it spanned a web of chains, keeping her motionless. The smoke began to clear enough for light to flood in. The web of shadows looked brilliant against the steel. They weren't stealing her, it was a hit.

There was blood, and she was going to die if I didn't act fast. Without realizing it, I had my locket in my hand and was holding it tightly. I stuffed it back in my shirt and tried to forget that asshole. If there wasn't a reward, I was going to be pissed. As I jumped into the hole, I was hit with the powerful scent of blood.

I grabbed onto the chains and began pulling, but they wouldn't budge. She hung motionless, moaning frequently, and I tried to think of a way to get her out. As I looked for a way to free her, I found something I wasn't expecting. A shard of metal, cold and wet to the touch stuck in her gut. I could feel a steady flow of blood coming out.

I wasn't a doctor and had no idea how to help her. The only thing I could do was break her free. The chains had to come off. The spiderweb-like shadow they had once cast began to twist and buckle. One by one they snapped, and she fell as the last of them broke.

I managed to catch her in time and lifted her into my arms. She struggled, which made it all the more difficult, and the doors were locked, obviously. I kicked at them repeatedly, drawing deeper inside for strength. Eventually, they flew open with the top bouncing around until it dangled above us.

The bottom one dropped like a ramp, and I ducked to get her out of there. Once on the ground, she was impossible to keep a hold of, wildly tossing herself to get free.

"Stop!" I shouted, surprising her, "I'm trying to help. You've got a chunk of metal in your side, you're bleeding to death. If you stop, I can get you out of here before the suits wake up. Then, maybe save your life."

She didn't speak but stopped struggling, and I put her on her feet. She could barely keep her balance, which meant I had to do the heavy lifting. I tried to remove the bag from her head, but it was chained to the collar. As I pulled, a small tear formed, revealing her right eye, at least she could see. That would make things go smoother, even with her hands still cuffed behind her.

It might have been bad because she instantly freaked when she saw me. Her mouth must have been covered in tape because all she did was mumble. The eye I saw told me everything, she looked at me as if she saw a hideous monster. I grabbed her arm, but she wiggled free and ran faster than I would have been able to in that condition.

"I may be out of makeup..." I screamed, "But I know I look better than your scrawny ass!"

There was a series of loud bangs, and my first instinct was to duck and cover. Once I could think, I saw the gunfire from the group of suits standing at their opened car doors. The bleeding to death was a problem for her, but the gunmen were an immediate one. There were three in all, probably more inside. They must have been trying to retrieve her, or maybe to finish the job.

I had to get to her first, easy right, she was injured and bound after all. I bolted from cover and took a flesh wound to the arm, but more importantly, it ruined my jacket. It would surely leave a scar, but my jacket was worth two hundred dollars, Pre-Event! The dicks were going to pay, nobody messed with my clothing, but the woman came first. I waited for them to reload and gave chase.

Watching her run reminded me of watching the blonde drunk run, but he was always faking. I could hear the bullets whizzing by as they fired a spray of them. I covered my head with my arms as she darted into an alleyway. They lost their line of sight, I could run without worrying about dodging a hail of bullets. I thought I'd lost her, but recognized the neighborhood and that alley was fenced off.

I let out a sigh of relief as I heard the roar of an engine. A sinking feeling fell into my gut as I turned my head and seen the suits from earlier in their car. There was no time to evade, I had noticed too late, everything moved in slow motion. The car slammed into my legs and pain surged through them. I bent over the hood at a weird angle, and I shot into the windshield head first.

The sound of the crunching glass sounded like bones breaking. I tried to protect myself, but I couldn't move. My body flipped up, bending my neck, and I slid across the roof of the car. I bounced off, spinning into the air. I landed hard on the ground, the side of my face smacked down first.

The concrete scraped across my skin like sandpaper. I had hit my head several times, but I swore I felt my brain disconnect on the last one. My nerves were on fire, and all my senses disorganized. The gunmen stepped over my motionless body into the alley.

There was nothing I could do, the alley was cut off by a chain-link fence, and the irony made me laugh. I had freed her from one set of chains only to be trapped by another. They pinned her against the fence as she screamed for her life behind the tape. They waved their guns in her face, throwing out dirty threats about what they wanted to do. Speaking vile things, and causing pain just to hear her scream.

With one hand in front of the other, I got back to my feet. It was more difficult than I imagined. Using the side of the building, I pulled myself up. My legs shook under my weight, but I stumbled forward. I was so pissed, they ruined my entire outfit and scuffed up my perfectly flawless skin.

I was going to kill every last one of them as violently as I could! As I walked, I dragged my right leg, and I could feel something inside me burst out in rage. It numbed the pain better than any drug could ever do and my strength flooded back. My vision was blurry, but it didn't stop me from going after them. At the end of the alley, I saw her back against the fence, hoping to step through it.

"Bitch, you've given the company a lot of trouble!" one gunman said, "You were told what would happen if you tried to escape again." I wobbled closer, keeping silent like a predator, "You've got no one to blame but yourself, Sera." and they raised their guns.

I stopped and raised my hand up, my palm facing out. I clenched my fingers down hard as if trying to squeeze something. The darkness began to stir, I felt it move, and the shadows shifted like a time-lapse video.

"Hey, assholes!" I screamed.

They turned to me and yelled inaudible slurs. I couldn't hear anything but the sound of my own heart. The shadows began dancing, eager to get their hands dirty. I stretched my fingers out like claws, with great tension against them as I curled them. With one final pull, I clenched my fist closed as they raised their guns in kind.

Large spikes of pure black shot from the shadows like needles, growing thinner the more they stretched. I impaled them like pin cushions with my shadow spikes. I had stopped them before a single shot was fired. There were so many sticking through their bodies, they couldn't move their fingers to pull the triggers. Their vitals were unharmed, I wanted them to suffer.

The harder I balled my fist, the more I pulled on the shadows. I was going to crush them all and pulled my fist back as hard as I could. The shadows resisted my demands, creaking like suspension cables. The alley walls shuttered and began to crumble under the force. The strain pulled my hand back, like pulling on a rubber band, but with a second yank, the spikes contracted. The walls caved, pulling toward the men, and the shadows fought to retake their original form.

Like a black hole, it was all sucked inward, crashing down atop them. A lot of excess rubble came tumbling down as I buried the bastards alive... for a moment.

"Yes!!!" said a deep voice with a pleased tone, almost fatherly.

I grabbed my head in pain as a second voice screamed, **"BrEAk THEir morTAL conSTRUCts and fEAST upON THEir iMMORtal Souls!"** with a young voice still cracking.

As their words stopped, the pain faded, but I still felt their murderous intent. I had no time to worry about the voices coming back again, I needed to stay on task. More goons were coming for her, I could feel them, I guess I had a few new playthings. Over the rubble, I barely saw her trying to worm herself over the busted fencing. With her hands still bound, she probably tore her wound more.

She rolled over and ran, desperation was the mother of motivation. I hopped after her with one leg dragging behind me. I clawed my way up the rubble and leaped off. I dropped over ten feet, landing on my legs with one hand on the ground. My chin nearly touched down, I felt like a frog.

My necklace had popped out of my shirt and my locket hit the asphalt. I looked at the puddle below and saw my face twisted in rage. It was damaged enough by the concrete, I didn't need early wrinkles too. I did my best to calm down and felt my face relax. I took off, hopping as I quickly stuffed my locket under my shirt while pulling my hurt leg behind.

She had a lead on me but hunting was my playground! The alleyway was littered with puddles, but there were also some big dry spots. She obviously ran to the end of the alley, but where had she gone after that? I followed the wet shoe prints out the alley, she had staggered closer to the building. She could barely run, her footsteps were erratic.

Soon, the footprints ended, but the blood trail didn't. She was bleeding badly, and who wouldn't? Bleeding like that, I had no idea how long she'd last. Her trail quickly cut the line of sight. I followed the trail down another alley, and through a narrow passage before coming back to the main street.

Her trail lead over her shoe prints, she had doubled over her tracks. The trail led into a park full of dead grass, she was trying to cover up the blood. She was good, she'd been on the run most of her life and would have lost most trackers. There was no way she'd lose me that easily, though. I finally spotted her, but a black car chased her into another alley, did they have a GPS tag on her?

There was no time to think about how they found her. That alley was a dead end, and I needed a better vantage point. From down the block, I climbed to the rooftops. All the buildings in the area were the same height, plenty of angles to work from. I used windows, pipes, and ledges to make my way closer. I found them kicking her on the ground, but I didn't have a clear shot.

After leaping across, one goon turned my way, "You guys see something just now?"

"What!?" the second said, "No, focus!"

He looked around a little more, "Swore I saw a shadow zip past." but he went back to kicking.

"Now, let's see what we can do with that pretty little face of yours. Bet I can carve a masterpiece into it!" the third and final guy said.

Suddenly, I whistled loudly from the rooftops, and they spun around. The last thing they saw was a flock of crows flying overhead, and they never knew what hit them. They watched the wings flap in unison, drawing them deep into a trance. Next, arrows rained down, killing them instantly. They fell, a quick, clean death, and I climbed down before more showed up.

I put my bow over my torso so I could get down, and ran to her once I knew the coast was clear. Using a knife I cut the bag from her head and removed her gag. The restraints were bound by a simple padlock. It was child's play, I would have expected more from a high-class bitch.

Once her arms were free, I rolled her over to look at her wound.

It didn't look good, she had to have been at the point of death. Messing with the wound must have shocked her awake. I knew it was a shock taking her knee to the side of the head.

I fell right into a puddle on my ass. Now, my ass was going to be wet all day, she was beginning to piss me off. I bounced back quickly and drew my knife on her.

"What the hell is wrong with you!?" I yelled, "I've done nothing but help you. The fuck!!!?"

"You stay away!" she held her wound with one hand and shook her finger at me with the other, "I see what you really are, monster. You can't fool me!"

I gestured to my wounds, "Don't call me names, bitch!"

"Don't screw with me, you know what I'm talking about!" she twisted her face with disgust, "You're one of them! You're all ugly, but you're the ugliest I've ever seen. You're something out of a horror movie. Corrupt politicians still look human, but your kind look like demons."

Did she know, or was she randomly accusing, "I'm tired of you running that mouth, bitch!"

"Stay away!" she screamed.

I went after her, she needed medical treatment, and maybe she had some information that would bring me a big payday. I was able to grab her, but she was full of surprises. She broke my grip and shoved her fist into my nose. It hurt, but it surprised me more than anything else and I punched her back by reflex. Even with a chunk of metal in her side, she fought back well.

It was like she wasn't injured, but it left her at a disadvantage. She kicked my knife into the air and dropped with a kick to my knee. I took my knife back after she tried to put it to my throat. I didn't know why, but I liked her! I slipped the knife away and bear-hugged her from behind. Followed by a suplex, something I had picked up from that man-whore, and I dropped her on her head.

She rolled around holding her skull as I stood up and adjusted my clothes. She swiped my leg out from under me, and I stumbled back. She ran at me and stuffed me into a trash can before I could recover. I felt her take my knife and heard something small hit the ground and she ran. I let her get one over me, I was so embarrassed I could have died.

It took a while to get out, and I pulled a rotten banana peel from my hair. In the distance, I felt someone watching me, but quickly noticed the tracking chip she'd removed with the knife. Now, on principle alone, she wasn't getting away from me...

DarkSide Chronicles: 2

I appeared on the rooftops before a bald, black man and a young man with red hair.

The red-haired man begged for binoculars from the other man, "Oh, come on, Torque!" he pleaded, "Let me see the catfight! Please, those chicks are hot!?"

"Not a chance Crank, besides, the fight's over." Torque was emotionless as he kept Crank back.

"No fair! You never let me use them!"

"And with good reason. You break everything you touch."

"Look, that only happened like once or twice, three times at the most."

Torque ignored his rambling and concentrated back on the black-haired woman who removed a banana peel from her hair. She pulled out a cloth to wipe her hands. She suddenly looked up, and if I didn't know any better, right at...

Torque for the first time showed a curious expression on his otherwise stoic face, "I swear the Goth one just looked at us." but his tone was less than emotional.

Crank rolled his eyes, "Oh, really now!? She spotted us from over two blocks away?"

Torque stood up, "Don't act like it's so unlikely. We've seen what she can do."

"Yeah! You know, you're right, I forgot. I did see that... with my binoculars! Yep, clear as day!"

"She pulled a bow from nowhere and struck them down with a storm of arrows by firing one. I think it's time we call the boss."

"Does that mean what I think it does!? Do we finally get a piece of the action?"

"We'll see what the boss says."

Torque pulled out a box and spoke into it, "... ... ... Boss, there's been a setback... No, the one from earlier. They didn't seem to know one another, but I think she's going to interfere with your plans. Yes, understood." and he put it away as Crank continuously gestured for an answer, "The boss wants us to take care of this matter personally."

"Yes! It's about time." Crank shouted ecstatically.

I had little interest in them, or what they did after. My interest lay with the woman, the one who was looking at me...

CHAPTER 18
LIKE A SAILOR

CLEARCREST, THE 27TH -- The Boy feared that the arrival of the biker only spelled out more trouble for him.

I kept asking myself who the hell that biker dude was, he came out of nowhere? Why was he fighting against a Sleeper, was he crazy? Before I knew it, that guy had already taken down the Sleeper and all the weird copies. He wasn't SAS, and even if he was, he'd turn on me just as fast. So, why was I still watching when I should have been running?

I needed to snap out of it before he spotted me, but I'd easily be seen. After the Sleeper had been defeated, the fog cleared, lifting the cover. A distraction would work if I could find a good place to hide. I had been hiding behind a garbage can, and I figured that would make a loud noise. I positioned myself to move to the new hiding spot and knocked it over.

His attention was drawn, and he came walking over. When the fog cleared up, I was screwed, otherwise, I would have kept hidden. The jacket the man gave me was huge and my breath was visible in the cold air. Still, if I hadn't acted I would have been caught, action was the only way to survive. My plan was good, but if he didn't come closer, it was useless.

That's when I noticed a pipe nearby and adapted it to the plan. Sure, I could have shot him and wasted a bullet, but he hadn't done anything to deserve that… yet. If I could hit him from behind, I could run while he recovered. I felt it was a good plan, after all, I could always draw my gun if I needed to. I grabbed it and ran at him as fast as I could without making noise and swung.

He heard me and turned around, only to get hit in the chest. My ankle twisted, causing me to stumble around, and I fell against the wall, bashing the back of my head. After that, it was all kinds of hazy, but I could still see him. It was weird, I thought, I could have sworn I heard him say something about his tit... I saw him unzip his leather jacket, and I was left speechless.

Dear mother of God those things were huge! How in God's name could I had mistaken her for a man!? Breasts aren't water balloons that would have flattened under pressure. I had dropped the ball on that one, and I was so distracted by my rambling thoughts I almost missed her undoing her helmet strap. She lifted it off, letting down long flowing auburn hair, and she had beautiful green eyes, like emeralds.

She pulled her shirt collar down to check the spot I hit under her bra, "Damn it, that's going to leave a bruise!" she said, rubbing the area, "Hey, you little cocksucker!" she shouted as she lifted me by my hair, "I just saved your ass, and this is the fucking thanks I get. Are you fucked up in the head, or do you just have something against women, you little shit!?"

She had the mouth of a sailor, the evil gaze of a demon, and the violent tendencies to match. No way she was a woman, she was too terrifying to be anything less than a monster!

"You messed with a wrong bitch, bastard!" and I began to fade, "Oh, don't you dare pass out! You better wake the fuck up, so I can beat your ass unconscious!"

Damn it, I had to get back up and run from her. I had to find Emi...

I yelled and yelled at the fucker, but it didn't do any good, he had passed out long ago. Venting my rage had its own rewards, but it didn't make my tit any less sore. The little ass had gotten me good, almost as good as the wall got him. Served him right, karma at its finest.

I had a job to finish, and I pulled out my phone and dialed, "... ... Yeah, I got him, just follow the GPS." and put my phone away.

It didn't take long before he came rolling up in his white pickup truck. I hopped down from a nearby car I had been sitting on and walked over to his truck, dragging the Sleeper behind me. He stepped out in his expensive shoes, fancy pants, and white silk shirt with the sleeves rolled up, even had a few of the buttons opened to show his chest.

"Really!?" I chuckled, "That's what you're wearing? I can't take you seriously in that. It makes me laugh every time I look at it."

He slid his glasses down, and glared over them, "If you're a thug, you dress like one, but if you're a businessman, you dress like a businessman." he was serious, but it looked like his normal face, "I don't run these streets anymore, I've moved up like you could have too."

"And wear a dress showing so much cleavage I might as well go topless, not happening!" I shook my head, "Besides, I'm a hands-on kind of person." and he frowned, "Oh, and only dicks wear shades at night."

I smiled as I lifted the Sleeper with one hand, hanging him out like a present. He remained cool, but I knew he was rolling his eyes on the inside. Silently, he flipped a switch and raised the back of his truck. Actually, it was the side, a modified bed of the truck. It was divided into two compartments that opened like car trunks but on the sides.

A mist flowed out, and I made sure not to inhale it. I had no idea what it was, but it was designed to keep Sleepers unconscious, and it was too strong to use on normal people.

He stepped back and said, "Okay, put him in." as he casually hid taking his shades off.

He acted big and tough, it was funny, but I'd never laugh, I wasn't crazy. I focused on the job and tossed the Sleeper in on his face to be done with it.

"There you go!" I dusted off my hands.

"Really?" he gave me a quizzical expression, "That's how we're going to treat your paycheck?"

I shrugged, "What, he can't feel it, well, at least not until he wakes up."

"They pay you to bring them back alive, and in one piece." he scolded me.

"Are you going to tell me who those people are, and what they're doing with all the assholes I catch?" he just glared, "Right, so I get to bring them back mostly alive, mostly in one piece, two at most, and you get to keep your business need to know."

He said nothing as he straightened the Sleeper up before shutting the compartment.

He pulled a wad of cash from his pocket, it was all nicely rolled, "Here's your pay."

"Thanks." I asked as I stuffed it in my jacket, "Oh, mind if I grab some supplies?" I said, gesturing to his trailer.

"Yeah, take what you need." he replied as he leaned against his truck.

His trailer was a camper redesigned to be a small store, like an ice cream truck for bullets. He was a man of connections, and inside was practically every weapon on demand. I liked to call it his house of pain... he didn't. As I collected ammo, I looked to see what else he had.

"So, who's the kid?" he asked me.

"The little shit hit me in the tit!" I said, rubbing the spot, it was still sore.

"A braver man than I, and you killed him for it?" he actually thought I killed the kid.

I poked my head out, "The cocksucker slipped and knocked his own ass out!"

"Sure he did." the sarcastic ass said as he looked away.

"Yeah, whatever!" I growled, "I took two 50 Cal clips, what do I owe you?"

"It's on the house." he said, waving it off.

I wasn't going to pass on free ammo, that shit was expensive in the current economy. After I was done, I closed up and slid my guns into the back my pants.

I looked down at the kid, "So, what about the kid, Chris?"

He shook his head, "I'm still looking for the two that never made it from the Airport. Best case, they died in the explosion, worse, they ended up like this kid." he said as he got into his truck, "I'm getting out of here, take care."

With that, he drove off, and I wasn't going to be too far behind him. I grabbed my helmet as I walked to my bike, but couldn't leave once I sat down. No matter how hard I tried, I couldn't bring myself to leave without making sure the kid was okay...

CHAPTER 19
THE LEAF SPRINGS SLAUGHTER

Oh God, what have I done!?....................................
...You got rid of what you didn't want anymore, like always...
........No, I loved you, I would never!...........Lies........

LEAF SPRINGS GAS STATION, FAIRWATER, THE 27TH -- The Angel of Silence didn't know it, yet, but the past would always come back to haunt her.

God, the pain was so strong! The visions woke me up, but I soon realized the pain was more real than it felt. I thought it was the vision, but it was my pain. I tried to open my eyes, but they were stuck together, and the right one hurt so bad! The left opened enough to see my clothes covered in blood and my wounds.

I was bruised and cut, there wasn't a part of my body that didn't hurt. The pain was so bad that I didn't notice that I was bound to a chair for a moment. I was scared and had no idea what was going on. Pulling against the restraints hurt even more, they were too tight.

"Wow!" someone said, "I've never seen someone unconscious thrash around like that."

I tried to speak, but all that came out was a mouth full of blood.

"Yeah, you're probably not going to be able to talk, or see for the matter." he said, "So, let me shine some light on this confusing situation. You're confused, right!?" he walked up behind me putting his hands on my shoulders, "Yeah, you're confused, so let me tell you. We're the fuckers you attacked earlier, you Sleeper bitch!" and he hit me over the head.

I had a splitting headache, but that made my head ring. It hurt to think, but I figured they were the bikers from the bar. They had pushed me over the edge once, there was no way they were going to survive!

"Do you have any idea how long we laid there, trapped in our own bodies, huh!?" he snarled, "Long enough to think of exactly how I was going to make you pay. I had some of the boys keep an eye out for you while the boss had them out looking for the drunk in the trench coat. That should pretty much connect the dots to here, and I'm sure as you can tell, we had some fun with you while you were asleep, whoa!" he screamed, "But don't get worried, we didn't have that kind of fun!"

He started prodding the back of my head with his, with his, I couldn't even think about it, "We like getting our dicks wet as much as the next guy, buuuuut… Well, we weren't sure if that Sleeper condition of your was anything like an STD! Am I right, boys!?" they cheered back.

I had to get out of there, but I couldn't struggle out of my restraints. I was so afraid, and the pain had already been overshadowed by the feeling of my heart sinking into my gut. They would all die if I didn't get out of there! Trying to break the restraints only rocked the chair.

"Oh, you're not getting away!" he yelled, kicking me in the chest, and I felt like coughing up a lung as chair tipped back.

I bashed the back of my head on the floor, but my ribs hurt most of all. My whole body was in such pain, I hadn't noticed my ribs were broken. Then it happened, the veil broke, faster than it ever had before, and there was nothing I could do about it. I couldn't fight the tears any more than I could fight against the bonds that held me. Any moment, something would come through and slaughter them.

I didn't want them to die, and it hurt me more inside than any physical pain. I had lost my will to fight as he lifted the chair back onto its legs. He stabbed a knife into my leg, it hurt so much, the nerves were already raw. I couldn't see more than blurry shapes, but I could tell it missed anything vital. This wasn't their first time, all the wounds were superficial to keep me alive and in pain.

"There, have a knife." he laughed, "You want out, go ahead, cut the ropes."

He was laughing, they were all laughing, how could people find torturing someone funny? They were monsters, this world would be better off without their kind. It was one thought that slipped into my mind, and it was all that it took. One slip and my hatred lured an unholy beast through the torn veil, and our world felt the effects. I heard things begin to fly all around as they panicked.

"What the hell are you doing, bitch!?" he screamed, and I saw vague blurs jumping around.

They came at me, but my chair began to lift into the air and slammed back to the floor. Before they knew what had happened, the chair slid backward, dragging me to the back of the room to safety. I could feel the heat of its claw against my skin, I knew which one had come. It was him again, oh God no, it was him, and he was going to kill them all just like last time. I heard their screams as I remembered the horrors of that night.

I felt the floor give under him as his weight actualized itself in our world. The shelves let out a screech as they bent and broke against his increasing volume until they tipped. I had to save them, he was going to slaughter them, but how could I escape from a chair? Thinking under pressure was never my strong suit, and my hands shook violently. I had to do something, I didn't want to remember it otherwise.

Maybe the chair would break if it fell again, I tossed my body back and forth until it tipped. When the chair rolled over, I bashed my head again. My vision faded, and their screams sang me to sleep as I passed out and everything around me went black…

I could still hear them screaming as I came to, I had only passed out for a moment. When I fell, though, my hand had been holding onto the arm of the chair and was smashed under it. No bones broke, but the pain to the already tender meat was excruciating. I pulled my hand from under it, getting my fingers pinched as they slide out. I was screwed, my only hope was to free my arm.

As I laid there looking at my hopeless situation, I saw the knife, maybe if I could get it. I extend my hand as far as I could, but I couldn't reach it. My legs were still bound, but I tried twisting it, it hurt, but not as much as my ribs lying like that. Getting one finger on the blade was enough to bring it closer, but realized I was wrong. The knife digging around in my leg as I wiggled it around was so much worse.

I could hear the bikers firing their guns at him and screaming as the bullets bounced off. I had to move quickly if I was going to save them and yanked as hard as I could. It came out halfway, it was too painful to do again. I listened to their screams and searched deeper for the strength to do it as I ripped it out on the second try. I wanted to scream from the pain, but I held it together and turned the blade to the ropes.

It was at a weird angle as I started to move it back and forth. Their screams motivated me to move faster, reminding me of what would be lost if I didn't hurry. I couldn't see the rope clearly, I just hoped I was making progress. The knife began cutting into my skin, I flinched, but gritted my teeth and kept slicing at the rope. I heard one scream out, then came a loud thud and gurgle as he went silent.

He had already got one of them, and my hand moved faster. I heard another scream, a splatter, and finally, his body hitting the floor. He was taking his time killing them, torturing me, forcing me to listen as he killed them. The rope cut, but the knife slipped from my hand. It slid away but was still well within reach if I could move my arm far enough with my broken ribs.

I got the rope off and tried moving my arm, but my body lit on fire with pain. My arm was pinned under my body, and I didn't have the strength to lift myself off of it. I had to keep wiggling it until it was out from under me. It was like trying to twist your arm in an unnatural way and feeling the muscle and bone strain. After a moment, my body dropped and pain surged through my ribs.

There was nothing I would let stop me as I reached out with my ribs crying in pain. I got my hand on the knife and made quick work of freeing my other hand. After that, I began releasing my legs, but I heard him take the life of a third one. Every time I heard one of them die, it felt like a piece of myself was getting ripped out. I was completely free, but getting up was a different story.

Moving an arm or two and sliding around on the floor was easier than lifting the weight of my entire body. Everything that had hurt before was clawing at me all at once, digging deeper than ever. I struggled to get to my feet and saw the flames. It was playing out as it had before, his flames would consume everything he didn't. Fighting harder, I put everything into standing, almost falling again.

Once up, I didn't need the strength and nearly threw myself back to the floor before I was even up. As I stumbled around, I clung to anything I could, eventually burning my hand on metal. It was nothing compared to what I was already feeling, and the pain vanished as quickly as it came. Luckily, I held on long enough to get my balance and began wobbling toward the screams. Everything was blurry, I had to take it slow with my hands out feeling around.

Not that I could have moved faster if I wanted to, my body was running on fumes. I saw a biker, I couldn't tell who it was, but I put my hands out trying to reach him in time. At the last second, I thought he had turned toward me, or maybe away from me to run. Even without my vision, I knew what blood splattering on my face felt like, and the fuzzy form of a head popping off its body looked like. God no, if I had been quicker, I could have saved him, now, he was gone.

At that moment, I thought they were all dead, but I heard one of them moan. I followed his groaning and swore I saw one on the floor behind the counter.

I stumbled around, bashing into the wall, and he screamed, "You get the hell away from me, you Sleeper bitch!" it was the one who stabbed my leg.

He raised his arm at me, and I heard a clicking noise repeatedly, he must have been firing an empty gun. I put my finger to my mouth to tell him to be quiet, but he drew attention from HIM. The monster threw itself on the counter, and I dove on top of the biker using my body as a shield. He roared for a moment before backing off, and I lost track of him.

"What in hell are you doing!?" the biker said, "Did you just save me!? You're doing this aren't you, why would you save me!?"

I put my finger to my mouth again, and the other to his mouth trying to get him to be quiet.

When he stopped, I pointed to the front door, but he stopped me, "I don't know what your game is, trying to save the people who were going to beat you to death, but I can't move." he said in a hushed tone, "My leg…" I quickly moved my hand around until I felt the bones sticking out of his leg, and he hissed, "Are you fucking stupid, bitch!? That hurts!" he grunted.

He wasn't going anywhere on his leg like that, at least not by himself, however, he could with my help. Gritting my teeth at the pain from my ribs, I dropped his arm over my shoulder. It felt like a ton of bricks hitting me, it felt so heavy as I tried to move.

"Are you mad!?" he snapped at me, "You can barely lift yourself, there's no way in hell you're walking me out of here."

He was right, even in full health, I lacked the physical strength to lift him up, but I had to try. With all my might, I tried to stand, but it felt like my heart was ripped out before my very eyes as that thing came through the wall. The wall exploded, but all that could be seen were wood chips bouncing off of something that wasn't there. It bit down, pulling him through the hole, and I lost my grip. I threw my arms out, grabbing a hold of his legs, but he suddenly came back through with too much ease.

Before I could think, my hands were already reaching through to pull him back through, but... All my fingers grabbed onto was his warm, gooey insides, because he'd been ripped in half. They were all dead, I'd failed to save a single one of them, and like before I was left alone with that thing. It was a horror show, my pale hands were darkened by his blood in my blurry vision. I could barely see, but it sent chills through my body, and I would have vomited if I had eaten anything in the past week.

I was scared, alone, and I needed to run, but I could barely stand. I wobbled as fast as I could from behind the counter and made a beeline for the front door. That's when I slipped in the puddle of blood pooling next to the biker who lost his head. I was thrown to the floor and froze. The wind had been knocked out of me, and the pain was overloading my senses.

I lay motionless as I looked up at the ceiling. While I gasped for air I couldn't help but cry. Why was I cursed to lose so many people? Then I felt its claws clutch around my body. I was gently lifted and set on my feet as I felt its searing hot breath on my neck.

It put me down, whispering something in a language I couldn't understand. With a laugh that sounded the same in any tongue, it faded through the veil, and the tear healed. I was left standing alone in a bloodbath, and I wondered if it made me a bad person wishing I wasn't alone. Even if that beast was the only one to keep me company, I didn't want to be left alone. The sprinklers came on, and I dropped to my knees crying as the stinging cold water washed the blood away.

I completely lost track of the outside world as I sat there. My mind shut down at the sight of the blood until the water had washed me clean. Maybe it was the police lights flashing that broke my trance. Before I could go anywhere, I tore a strip of bandage from my leg and wrapped it around the knife wound right above it. I'd be labeled a Sleeper for what happened that night if they caught. So, I never looked back as I ran away, but I'd never forget...

CHAPTER 20
WHATCHA SELL'N

FAIRWATER, THE 27TH -- The Silver Bullet returned to the scene of the crime with confidence.

I walked into the store, where broken glass lay strewn across the carpet. A long tear divided it like a heavy object had been dragged through. This was no condition for a fine seller of porn to keep their establishment.

I approached the fine lass as she swept the glass, "What happened?" I asked as I poked her in the shoulder harder than necessary, "You should be ashamed of letting this place go!"

"Wait a minute!" she leaned in, "You're the dickhead who came in here on the boat dressed like a Viking and stole most of our stock!"

I shook my head, "Dear child, I, nor my outrageously large mustache knows what you're talking about." I said as I stroked my manly stache vigorously.

"You are!" she screamed as she ripped away my mustache.

My poker face was ruined only by the low hissing that escaped my mouth for some time. I had super glued it to my face, but I held steadfast against the agonizing pain. The red-hot, searing agony made my nose hairs curl, my butt pucker, my toes clench, and my fingers squirm. Instead of showing weakness… I screamed like a little girl, "Aaaaaaaaaaaah!!!" while making the weirdest face imaginable.

"Oh my God!" she shouted loudly, "Did you bring them back with you!?"

"Even if I were this handsome man you speak of, why would I be stupid enough to keep the damning evidence on me…" I said as I patted my bulging coat as Santa would his belly.

"Oh, really!" and she retrieved a DVD from my trench coat.

"E-gad!" I screamed, "What sorcery is this!? Do your hands not generate porn at a whim? You lass bring new beauty to this dull world!"

There was an awkward silence as she gave an evil glare, I tell you, I felt my soul crush a little. I screamed like a wild man to throw her into a state of bewilderment before grabbing the DVD. I waddled from her with great haste and made a mad dash for the backroom. There, I made my great escape through a long-hidden secret passage. I'm sure she was scratching her head at my Houdini trick.

Upon following the long staircase to the bottom, I found myself in the underworld of Fairwater. A place where merchants sold an assortment of things. For the right price, one could find guns, intel, and the ever rare bunny girl! It was a place for all sorts of unsavory people to gather, and you had to be to know about this place, not that I... The red carpets, tall pillars, and gold everything made the place really pop out in the candlelight!

I was there to find something new and spicy to get my hands on. A familiar face was selling firearms.

As I ran to him, I yelled, "Yo, Mac, whatcha sell'n!" with a raspy accent.

He turned in his usual overalls and said with great joy, "Ah, it's always a pleasure to see you, my boy! Have I ever told you, you're my best customer?"

"Mac, tell me what you've got." and I leaned against the counter with one arm.

He said with a sad expression, "Sorry, I don't have anything new."

"Oh well! Give me the usual!"

"That's what I like to hear!"

A moment later, he came carting out a wheelbarrow with enough firepower to last me... a day or so. To complete the exchange, I recovered a suitcase of cash from my trench coat. Mac's eyes lit up as they always did, and I wheeled away my loot while I whistled a merry tune.

A large, familiar, black man stopped me shortly after, "You dropped your… Dynamite!" he said with a worried look.

I turned with a blank stare, "You seem familiar… Are you the queen of England? No, wait, don't tell me!" I pressed my finger over his lips far enough to invade his personal space, "You're a giant man bear, no, a giant black man, no, a tiny black man pretending to be a giant black man. Chris, it's you!" and I hugged him.

He wore his normal unchanging expression of complete disdain, "Don't touch me." and he picked me up like a small child and set me down.

I stood silently before I snatched the dynamite, "Thanks for spotting that, I don't know what I'd have done without her, she's one of a kind." I said as I wildly waved her with erratic gestures, "Dyna has an explosive temper, my ears would have been blown off." he appeared worried as I waved her.

I lifted the tarp that covered my stuff and threw her into a crate of ninety-nine completely identical sticks of dynamite.

"Shit, boy!" his eyes nearly bulged out of his head, "Are you preparing for the zombie apocalypse!?"

"NOOOO…" I said with a goofy smile as I waved my hand, "That was so last year, killer zebras are all the rage now! I've just got a few essentials… Twenty-five containers of nitroglycerin, sixty bricks of C4, thirty frag grenades, a baker's dozen Molotov cocktails, a hand full of thumbtacks, machine guns, submachine guns, assault rifles,

rocket launchers, and a red stapler with a big pink ribbon…
I swear, I'm just holding it for a friend!" I said with a
serious expression.

Chris gave me a quizzical stare, "What, are you
raiding porn stores dressed as Vikings again?"

I grabbed his head and pressed my face side by side
to his, "Who told you that!? I know nothing… You've seen
nothing. YOU'VE SEEN TOO MUCH!!!" I screamed.

I retrieved Dyna and prepared to unleash her fiery
temper to make my getaway.

Chris squeezed out the fuse, and put it back in the
crate, "I'm leaving before you get us killed." and he walked
away before he looked back briefly.

"Good thinking," I said, "Plausible deniability.
Goodman!" I said as I tapped my head with Dyna.

He had a very serious look about him, "Word on the
street is Salvatore's boy has been taking over the east
bracket and is working with Father Patrick. He's a hotshot
if you know what I mean, and I want you to stop harassing
the Church before you get the city burned down! Got it!?"
and he gestured he was watching me.

I mulled this over, "… Want some fish?"

He glared harshly, and I ran away with my wheel
barrel. Now that I had my weapons of destruction, it was go
time! I couldn't take any more of its mockery, it had to go!

"That's it, I've had enough of your sass!" I
screamed as I dramatically pointed to the church.

Dark storm clouds hovered over and thunder
rumbled as if accepting my challenge. I narrowed my eyes,

hoisted my pants higher, and charged the main doors. My foot struck the door with all my drunken rage, and it shattered beneath my fury. Actually, it didn't break, but I did get a stubbed toe. It may have had the first laugh, but I would piss in their holy water in due time.

I reached into my bag of tricks, aka, my trench coat with pockets more endless than Santa's bag. From within, I pulled out everything I had, and I was armed with so many guns, it was like I was wearing them as armor. I held two assault rifles ready to open fire when blood dripped from the eyes of the decorative knockers. As I looked into their eyes, I could see an evil that pierced my soul. My resolve had been lost, fear consumed me, and I got out of there... PSYCH!

I ran back full speed with my army helmet strapped on and dove at the door. It thought it could stop me with fear, but I showed it I didn't understand anything! My head threw open the doors, and I came to a stop, epically posed like a turtle stuck on its back. All the guns were weighing me down, but some expertly maneuvered wiggles got me to my feet locked and loaded.

The occupants went into a panic when I fired off several rounds into the air, and I screamed my demands, "Okay, this is a holdup..." wait, that didn't seem right, "No, this isn't Tuesday. I'm here for your women..." that felt right but seemed off topic, "No, that's not right either. I'm here for your communion wine, then, your lives!" there wasn't a single part of that statement I didn't like, "Yeah, that's the one!"

The priest raised his hands and just like that, he calmed congregation, "My dear boy, you are in the House of God. Leave now before you are stricken by the Lord's divine wrath.

"Screw you and your dress!" I screamed, "I'm here to kick some religious, fanatical ass!"

The priest was not happy with my words. His face remained calm, but I could see it in his eyes.

"How dare you act like a heathen in the House of God." he turned to the worshipers, "This non-believer has the audacity to disrespect our Lord and bad mouth our faith. He's the devil that walks amongst us, a vile Sleeper. God is testing us by sending the beast to our doorstep. We must sacrifice him to the Lord Almighty to gain entrance to Heaven."

I smirked, "I don't think so, dress man! Your evil ends here on this fine Saturday afternoon."

The priest opened his mouth and I saw him for what he was, a demon in a man's skin. His mouth was full of razor sharp teeth, his screams an ungodly roar, and the worshipers became demons. Finally, we could end the stupid charade and get down to business. I raced toward them with guns aimed forward, but I moved slowly. Everyone looked on in confusion, these guns were heavier than I thought.

Suddenly, some force rushed my feet, tripped me, and caused me to fall right onto my knee.

As soon as I hit the floor, a burden had been lifted, and I could move freely again, "Oh your God, oh your

God!" I screamed as I held my knee and hissed, "My knee, ow, ow, ow!" I jumped back to my feet, "Okay, it's go time!"

I ran for the priest again when two secret service fellows stepped from behind him. They were like a folded up piece of paper someone had cut, and from them unfolded a string of men in black suits. To make matters worse, a giant ball of cheese, probably cheddar dropped before the priest and rolled toward me. Instead of running, I fell to my knees with a terrible shrill as I looked upon my cheesy doom. The cheese ball passed over me, I was unharmed.

I jumped to my feet and laughed, "Oh, yeah, I forgot. Oops!"

The priest motioned his hands, and the assembly charged me. They were a joke, each only took a couple of bullets, the lightweights couldn't hold their lead. I could have regaled the masses for years with my quick work of the lesser ones, but there were more pressing matters. Only the demon priest and goons in black remained, and I'd finish them quickly. The priest's face twisted with a demonic smile, and his human skin stretched as something moved underneath.

Before I could unleash my fury, the priest gestured, and his goons hopped forward. They jumped like grasshoppers barely bending their legs, but jumped very high. They ascended slowly as if floating but fell quickly like gravity had suddenly increased. I was overrun and had my butt handed to me in a decorative hand basket comprised of chocolates, cheeses, and fine meats. An uppercut nearly tossed to the ceiling, and my jaw felt like it had been abused by a chair.

I fell outside, surrounded by glass after what felt like a kick sent me through a stained glass window. I was in a backyard filled with vibrant, green grass lined with glass shards. For a moment, I laid there and looked at the sky as the clouds drifted by with a gentle breeze against my face. I contemplated important topics, government control over the masses, religious freedom to take others' freedoms, and if cute cat videos would one day rule the internet completely. All very important, but they were only useful for clouding my mind.

My feet crawled underneath me, they dug their way into the dirt and forced me to rise. I thought I was back in the fight, but I was whacked in the face by a rack. I stumbled back as I held my bloodied nose and found myself in a diabolical trap. I had fallen into a circle of rakes, different directions yielded the same results and more nose pain. There were a plethora of hypotheses I tested, from jumping, running, flipping, rolling, even reading them bedtime stories, but nothing stopped their ceaseless attacks.

I'd had enough, it was time to solve the problem the one way I knew I could. As it came for my nose, I whipped out my trusty sawed-off and shot it. I would have rejoiced had I actually won, but instead, I was hit in the balls by the now shortened rack. I fell to the ground holding myself as my lips twisted, and my eyes tried to escape their sockets.

With a scream, I jumped to my feet and teleported out of the circle to destroy each rack with my bare hands.

Once the deed was done, I teleported back and casually strolled out unharmed.

I broke it down into a little dance, "Yeah, take that you stupid rakes! Yeah, that's right, I'm smarter than a rake."

My dancing felt right, but it was no time to celebrate, I had a priest to excommunicate. I ran to the church exterior, diving at the wall and passing through it. I would have stuck the landing, but a stand jumped out of nowhere and stood there... mocking me. I tripped over it and doused myself in holy water.

I began screaming in agony, "Oh your God, it burns, it burns so bad!" I held my fist up, clenching it, "I need my magic elixir."

I calmly searched a nearby cabinet until I found a bottle of wine. I downed that bad boy and leaped to my feet with new found strength coursing through my veins. That's when I noticed the priest and his thugs were gone, but suddenly, the paint peeled from the walls and ceiling the ripped away. Above was a seemingly infinite space of sickening colors swirling aimlessly, and from behind the walls rose the priest. He was massive and looked like a true demon still cloaked in his girly white dress.

The men in black flooded in, crawling across the walls on all four with their heads turned backward. The final boss fight stood between me and victory, it was go time! I teleported around the room and evaded gunfire while returning my own. The intensity of the battle grew with each passing second. I had to up the ante and switched my assault rifles for my 50 Cal machine gun.

Screw recoil, gravity, and logic, I ran on the walls busting some caps. When I shot one, they'd exploded into blood like a water balloon popping. I found myself a nice, narrow corner to get surrounded in and pulled out my flamethrower to roast some suits! As the last one burned alive, the priest caught me by surprise in his grasp. He screamed in agony and dropped me along with my thumbtacks.

I jumped back armed with a rocket launcher, "Where's your god NOW!?" I shouted.

The explosion shattered the priest and his former self fell to the floor before me.

I put a magnum to his forehead, "I've got a bullet with your name on it."

The priest begged for his life, "No, stop, I beg you. Pray unto the Lord and your sins will be forgiven."

My eyes narrowed and responded with a witty remark, "Ahdf asdgdsih aidshgsd gihadsg." man I cracked myself up.

"What now!?" the priest looked confused.

I rolled my eyes, "Fagsdhisd agsdhi gsdhagsd isoeoeg!" but his confusion seemed to deepen, "Rtghhjmkklllllll..."

Suddenly, my mouth hung open foaming. The wine must have been spiked, tainted by religious nutbaggery! I fell over convulsing as I ran in circles of the floor, still foaming at the mouth. Reality broke and I faded with it...

DarkSide Chronicles: 3

The man in black watched from a building ledge as he always did. Law enforcers ran into an old, run-down building called a "Doughnut Shop" only to fly out the windows. The shop was riddled with holes from their mechanical hand devices, was on fire, and inside a man in a long silver coat was on a rampage. A homeless man hid with a hole through his hat, the bullet damaged little more than his hair. The silver coat was a wild man, foaming at the mouth, and his words were gibberish.

His actions were insane, and he'd escape capture by biting or poking them in the eyes. They fired these strange tubes into his butt, and eventually, his movements slowed, but he was still a challenge. Soon, he could fight it no longer and fell to the ground convulsing.

They approached as he shook wildly, "Move in very slowly, we don't want to spook him."

They surround this man, but he became frightened. His struggle was in vain, for all he could muster was running in circles on the floor. They couldn't get a firm grip and decided to pile on top of him instead. With their combined might, they restrained his wrists and ankles with shackles. Still too unruly, they tied him up from head to toe with anything they could find.

By wriggling like a worm, he broke free and flopped like a fish out of water. Six men in all were required to carry him out, and they threw him into the back of a strange carriage.

The man in black placed his hand on his face, and shook his head, "Why did I think it was a smart idea to talk to this one?" a boot came to a rest on the ledge next to him.

A male voice spoke, "I told you talking would be pointless. He lives in his own little world, all he knows is his reality. The only way to get through to him is with violence." the man remained out of view, I never saw his face, "On that topic, I only joined you because I was promised payback, but all you seem interested in is this stupid game."

"Everything has a time and place. Building up the suspense is what makes a story good."

"And never getting to the end is a sure-fire way to ruin it!"

The man in black sighed, "Why can't you enjoy his pain and suffering like a good little homicidal maniac, huh?"

"Fun and games are for little kids... He and that bitch cost me my childhood a long time ago. All that's left is the rage, and it wants his blood." he fidgeted with a thin piece of paper with a "J" and symbol similar to an arrowhead.

"Everyone seems to be misunderstanding the whole point of these little excursions." the man in black said as he stood, "If you can't behave, I'll send you back early like her."

"I know how to play my part. A soldier follows orders, and besides..." he paused briefly, "the one in bright purple, she creeps me out."

"You know about that tongue trick of hers?" the man in black asked with a smile.

"Yes..." the other man became angry, "and I wish Ashia hadn't told me." he sounded disgusted, "So, drop it!"

The man in black put his hand to his head and laughed as they walked away and vanished into darkness...

CHAPTER 21
WATCHING FROM THE SHADOWS

F41RW4T3R, UNK0WN -- The Shadow Diva stalked Sera from a distance.

She walked through town as she blended with crowds. She must have thought all of us were following her via the tracking chip because she wasn't in a hurry now. She kept her wound hidden under her jacket, not like anyone would have cared anyway. I kept my distance, there was no reason to make her think otherwise if she thought she lost me. I was able to keep an eye on her from the shadows.

I followed her to a pharmacy, she was going for first aid supplies. Her wound was too bad for a simple treatment, what was she thinking? She left a trail of blood dribbling on the tiles as she slumped down the aisles. She was getting worse, she'd gone pale. She stole gauze and anything else she could.

She stuffed it all into her jacket, but she could barely stand. She was getting woozy and couldn't keep her eyes open. How was she going to help herself? Out of the corner of my eye, I recognized a symbol on the window, the Black Suns. Great, she was stealing from a gang with one foot in the grave already.

I thought she was clear, but a big, bald Asian man came from the back room. He walked up to an American guy behind the counter and whispered. Then they both looked at her, the cameras! He must have seen her stealing from the security room. How could I warn her without making her run again?

Running would probably kill her if the big guy didn't get to her first. He was loaded with tattoos, and I spotted a pistol that stuck out of his pants. What was it with guys sticking loaded weapons down the front of their pants!? Luckily, she spotted him and was nearly perfect at acting like she hadn't. She moved away in character and went toward the side door.

He hadn't noticed yet, I was impressed with her skill. She kept her composure and left the building. As soon as she bolted out the door, he grabbed her. He pushed her to the ground as the door closed. I reached around from behind and grabbed his gun.

With one motion, I popped the safety as I aimed the gun inward and pulled the trigger. His pants filled with blood as he fell screaming, I probably blew his dick off. I kept his gun and blended with the shadows. She took one look and ran again, and as soon as the coast was clear, I scooped up what she had dropped and went after her. The others would be out any second, she had no choice but to run.

She was getting worse, staggering like a drunk. I knew she wouldn't be alive much longer. I was surprised that she hadn't gone into shock yet. She covered ground fast, and eventually, slipped into an old residential area. Most of the houses had been boarded up and fenced off during the months after the Event. They quarantined houses off wherever there was an infected, hoping to stop the spread.

She stopped in front of one such house. First, she made sure no one was watching and slipped through a broken area of the fence. Once on her hands and knees, she couldn't stand, so she crawled under the house. From a crawl space, she entered a hole under the house. The house above was dark and trashed.

The only light coming in was from a window at the top of the steps. Using the rungs of the rail, she pulled herself up one step at a time. I noticed every window had thick clothes over them except the one, which had fallen. At the top was a hallway with a rickety door barely on its hinges. She dragged herself into the room that lay beyond and went to the bed.

She fumbled in the darkness until she lit a lighter. I hid from the light as she lit a candle sitting on a dirty dresser. The room looked like it had been tossed many times. There was a tiny rocking horse and a small bed with torn sheets and blankets. Crayons littered the floor with many pictures, all drawn poorly, it was a child's room for sure.

She emptied her pockets onto the bed and began frantically looking for something. She flipped things repeatedly, hoping it would magically appear somewhere she had already looked. Clearly, she was looking for what she dropped, so I placed in the room. I left it as close to her as I could while staying in the shadows. When she realized it wasn't on the bed, she looked to the floor and spotted it.

She lifted her shirt above her abdomen, tearing it on the metal shard. She threaded a needle and sterilized it in the fire before she grabbed the metal. With one powerful yank, she ripped it from her stomach and gushed blood. It was almost unbearable the way she screamed as she pulled it out. Without hesitation, she rammed her fingers into the wound.

I was no doctor, but she seemed like she'd done it before. There was no way I could help, or she'd run again. Hopefully, there was a good payday in my future if she managed to pull through. Then I heard something small hit the floor and tilted my head in for a look. She was hunched over against the bed with her arms hanging limp.

The needle she had been using was barely scratching against the floor as it hung from the thread.

I looked closely at her, I couldn't tell if she was breathing, but she wasn't moving, "Shit!"

There was no dancing around it now, I had to see if she was still alive. Her body was motionless, it didn't look good. I placed my fingers to her neck, but a heartbeat never came. She was dead, and I felt sorry for her even if the bitch had punched me in the nose. No normal person could have held in as long as she did, she was a fighter.

I had only seen one other person that determined to live while kicking Death's door, but hopefully, he was dead now. I didn't understand why she wanted to live so bad. She was a slave and her owner didn't care how badly she was beaten as long as she was returned. When I looked at her, I saw a torn and beaten woman hardened by misfortune, but I could sense very little darkness. If she really could see the true darkness within people, I knew how she felt.

People only see the tip of the iceberg. The truth is something so horrible that it should never be seen. All of it made me want to cleanse the Earth of that evil. I had to ask myself, was I going to be like them and leave her there to rot? I had to take care of myself, surviving was more important than caring for the dead.

If I didn't want to end up like her, I needed to take what I could and keep moving, the world was unforgiving. I grabbed a bag in the room and loaded it up with all the medical supplies. I put out the candle, and walked out of the room and left her...

CHAPTER 22
THE LORD'S LIGHT

FAIRWATER, THE 27TH -- The Angel of Silence cried out in tears louder than any words.

I wandered around the city for hours in the cold air, too scared to stop. It was so cold, I was so alone, and there was no person or place to run to. I couldn't go home, I didn't feel safe anywhere, so I kept walking. The cold was unforgiving, I was soaked to the bone, and my hands had already lost feeling. Then, like I was being punished, the sky roared.

Lightning ripped through the clouds and it began to rain. It seemed my punishment was to continue, and I deserved it. From what I had done there was no forgiveness, there was no repentance. I had the blood of their lives on my hands, and nothing would ever remove the stain of that sin. If it was God's will that I suffer for my transgressions, I would gladly accept any punishment. Suddenly, as if being guided by the hand of God himself, I stood before his house.

The church stood like a beacon of hope for those who were lost. The wind blew hard against my back, pushing me toward the doors. Could I have misread the Lord's signs as a punishment, while instead, he had been leading me toward shelter and maybe forgiveness? I prayed deeply with all my heart that I could be forgiven for the atrocities I'd committed, for the blood I spilled. I prayed that God would shine his light upon me and cleanse my sins.

I walked towards the church, but the storm grew strong, the winds grew violent and pushed against me as I walked up the steps. Even without the wind fighting against me, it was a near-impossible task to climb the stairs in my condition. Any muscle I hadn't been using to walk went weak in the cold. I had only my sight to rely upon as I walked up the steps for my feet had gone numb. Each step was a struggle, every push pulled me back down, it was a trial.

My body was heavy, every movement felt like an eternity. The stone steps were soaked and extremely slick. Halfway, I lost my footing and fell onto the stone, bashing my chest off them. The wind was knocked out of me, but my ribs killed me. The pain almost made me pass out and all the harder to breathe.

I crawled up the stairs, the cold stone stung as people came from the church. They walked past me like I didn't exist, and I didn't understand why they would do that. It was as if I was another part of the scenery, something you wouldn't give a second glance. Soon, they had gone, I was alone in the cold and rain again. I remembered the horrors I was running from and it gave me the strength to go on.

Eventually, I made it to the top of the stairs and found a column to grab onto. I lifted myself up bit by bit as I fought against the pain radiating from my ribs. I shuffled and dragged my feet as I walked toward the portal. The large wooden doors became a crutch as I fell against them. I felt them press upon every part of my body, they made me feel safe as I regained my strength.

In that instance of comfort, I thought I fell asleep, if only for a moment. Inside would be warm, I needed to get through before I blacked out again. The door was heavy, it was very solid, and wouldn't budge. I pushed and threw my weight into it, only to hurt myself more. After a few pushes, the door creaked as it opened.

When it finally opened, a burst of warm air hit me in the face. A soft light shined through the crack between the doors. I pushed it open far enough to squeeze through and had a hard time as I shut it behind me. I began to warm up quickly, with small chills jumping through me from wet clothing. I moved farther into the church, like a moth to the flame and stumbled along the way.

There were a few people there, but I found a pew in the back to myself. I curled up with my hands held in front of my face as I prayed. The things I had done, I was a horrible monster, and all their blood was on my hands. Praying didn't feel like it would ever wash away the sins. I could only hope that the Lord would forgive me, but how could I be forgiven for such crimes?

"How are you, child, you don't look well?" I hadn't noticed Father Patrick approach, "Child, it's okay, you're safe now." he used a finger to slide back the hood I had pulled tightly over my face, "Lately, more often than not you have been coming in here injured. This time doesn't seem as bad as usual, but getting hurt at all is bad."

He was not wrong, I came here a lot because of my curse and my responsibilities. I pulled away from him, I was uncomfortable around people, and I was ashamed. After scooting to the side, I pulled my hood back over my face.

"I don't even know your name, but I fear for your safety, child." he was concerned, "I keep you in my prayers, but one of these days I'm afraid you'll disappear and stop coming altogether. That you'll wind up dead somewhere and no one will ever find you."

Those words were never truer, but that's exactly why I was out there. It had been my responsibility since childhood, and I must see it through until the end. The work of the Lord had fallen to me, I'd been tasked with seeing it through as those before me. My only hope was that the Lord would forgive me for the lives I am unable to save while charged with these duties. Then for every soul I am unable to save when I am no longer capable of carrying out his will.

"Child, do you have a home to go to?" he asked and I nodded, "Is it nearby, child? You do not look as though you could manage a journey in your condition. Why not stay here for the night and venture out in the morning when the weather is more agreeable?"

I began to panic, I couldn't impose on him, especially after what I had done. I threw up my hands, waving them back and forth as I tried to tell him no, but he put my hands down.

"Nonsense, child, you should stay here for the night." he gave a kind smile, "We have rooms in the back for these exact situations?"

I didn't know how exactly to tell him no without being rude, I certainly wasn't worthy of his generosity. Before I could tell him no, the sound of the front doors closing caught my attention. I glanced over to see two men and a woman walking in. The first was a short, stubby man wearing a scarf, shades, and a fedora while smoking a cigar. I recognized him from somewhere, I had seen him, but couldn't place where.

The second was a very serious looking, tall, distinguished man, but he didn't look familiar. The third was a woman dressed like... what she was wearing was embarrassing. I felt dirty just looking at it, like I had to pray for her forgiveness. It looked like a long black coat buttoned down the middle, but it was a dress. It went down as far as the knees, but it was split up the sides of the thighs.

It made me feel like a thousand nuns would smack me with rulers just from seeing it. The moment I saw her, I turned away with my face lit up redder than a fire hydrant. Something about them caught Father Patrick's attention, and he stood and stared for a moment.

"I'll be back in a moment, child." then he walked to them.

I returned to my prayer as I tried to ignore them, but I could hear them talking. Not enough to know what they were speaking about, just bits and pieces. I focused my mind back on prayer, it was wrong to listen in on another's conversation. No matter how hard I tried to tell myself it was wrong, my ear kept going back to them. I only made out a few keywords.

Father Patrick said something about never coming inside, while the only other one who ever talked was the tall man. He spoke of something not being on time, and he was tired of waiting. I guessed from the way they dressed, they were very wealthy and probably speaking about money. The father said he'd have it ready soon enough, there had been some delays. There was a little more to it but in the end, the man said he'd wait longer, but he wasn't one to be screwed with.

They walked off and as they did, the woman shot me a glance and blew me a kiss. As soon as they had left, Father Patrick came back with a worried look on his face. They must have been a gang strong-arming him, it must have been so terrifying. The father had always been so nice to me, I couldn't stand aside if he was in need. So, I reached into my bag and grabbed all the cash I had and presented it to him.

He looked puzzled, "What's this child!?" he asked.

I motioned toward where they had been standing and pushed the money against him. It wasn't much, but hopefully, he could put it to better use than I could.

He quickly realized what I was trying to tell him, and he put his hands on my shoulders, "No child, that's not what that was about. You keep your money, dear." he smiled, "Now, put that away before someone sees it, and let's get you to a room. You look exhausted."

He walked me around the back of the church and lead me to a room. After turning down the bed, he told me if I needed anything to let him know, and I should get some sleep. That was the last thing I wanted to do right now, otherwise, the dreams would come again. The bed was warm, and my clothes were starting to dry. As hard as I tried, I couldn't stay awake and quickly drifted off curled up in the bed.

It wasn't long before the dreams started like I knew they would. I found myself in a house full of pictures with a couple in all of them. Scenes of a smiling man and woman filled my head, I could feel their happiness and love. Then things took a dark turn, I could feel death, terror, and rage. Feelings that were once so pure and innocent became twisted and corrupted.

Blood soaked my mind as pain and misery rushed through my body. Visions of the house and street flooded my sight like a trail of breadcrumbs. I woke up wanting to release every bit of the pain I had experienced in a scream that would never come. There was no way to know how long I had been asleep, but the sky was readying for first light. It couldn't have been more than an hour before day would break completely, and sleeping was out of the question.

Once I got those visions, they are in my brain like I had a photographic memory. The only way to expunge them was to solve the puzzle. Seeing such things was something I'd wish upon no one, I was a broken and cursed being. I couldn't help but think at times I must have done something unforgivable. The harder I tried to fight against it, the harder it pushed back.

The visions came continuously, increasing in intensity, and then the migraines would start. I'd lose the ability to sleep, I'd be unable to rest until their souls could. The human body can only take that kind of treatment so long before it gives. If nothing was done about it, I feared the worst. I'd avoid them for as long as I could, but I'd always cave in the end.

Soon the headaches would start, and I was already in enough pain. It had to be done quickly. I grabbed my bag and left for the street burned into my mind like a transparent image...

CHAPTER 23
WHAT HAPPENED IN CHERRY HILLS

CLEARCREST, THE 27TH -- Little Red was all the closer to an answer, but she would never catch the white hair.

It was raining again, I'd taken shelter under a bus stop booth. My legs were tired, I had them pulled up next to me on the bench as I sat. The only light to see by came from her soul. The surrounding street lights weren't getting power. She kept buzzing around me like an annoying gnat.

I sat there for twenty or thirty minutes before a bus came. Funny, I had only planned on waiting out the rain. Something was going my way, I could take the bus to a hotel. I forced myself up and walked to the bus door before it hissed and slid open. When I stepped in, I could hear and feel the metal sheets beneath my feet tapping the frame below.

The inside was well lit, but there were few people. Placing the money into the box, I moved to the back. A weird feeling came over me as I sat down, I curled up holding my rabbit. It was old, but even now it had the ability to calm me. Strange how things have such power over us.

I rocked for some time, but then, I finally noticed them. How had so many gotten on the bus without me realizing? A couple of the masked weirdos had followed me, but I didn't remember the bus stopping. Things were less than comfortable. Their heads turned unnaturally as they looked back at me with unbreakable gazes.

Then everyone else on the bus began putting on the masks. All of them, the same porcelain masks and their white coats. Incoherent mumbling came from behind their masks. My body was paralyzed with fear as they approached. Like a pack of zombies, they piled atop me.

I kicked and swung my fists, but I couldn't escape. I couldn't see or breathe, it felt like being strapped to a gurney. The harder I fought, the tighter I was constricted. Suddenly, my arms and legs were free, and I was flailing in an empty room. I scurried to the closest wall and looked around to see I was alone.

I had no idea where I was, but I ran for the door. No luck, it was locked, next was the window, but bars that covered it were solid. Then the glass exploded inward, and it flung me against the wall. The padding absorbed my impact, but my arm stung when I moved it. I grit my teeth and pulled a shard of glass from it and threw it to the floor.

The wound wasn't deep, nor was there much blood. I ignored the pain as I got to my feet, but that was all I could do. Only God knew where I was. That's when I heard the jingle of keys, and the door slowly creaked open. I wasted no time as I ran to the door.

I peered through cautiously and the hallway was empty. Then a shadow jumped across the wall, startling me, but I was more concerned that nothing had made it. I was the only one there, yet a shadow moved. The hall was otherwise dark except for enough light to make out shapes. I wasn't going to figure out anything inside the room, so I proceeded carefully.

I stepped through the door when it suddenly closed on top of me with crushing force. I couldn't breathe, it felt like someone was standing on my chest, but there was no one. Everything became a daze as I faded out, and the last image I saw was a shadowy figure watching from the end of the hall. I passed out and just as quickly found myself shackled to a chair with a bright light shining over me. The chair was cold and made of wood, the metal restraints pinched my skin, oh, and I was naked, that was weird.

My legs spread open and shackled to the chair legs, my arms to the armrests, and my head to the back of the chair. I scanned the room as best as I could with my head restrained. Repeating, metal like tapping echoed through the room in rhythm. I grew very nervous as things began moving just out of sight. I heard clacking against the floor, and it was moving toward me.

On the metal table with a cloth draped over it jumped a cat from the shadows. It was covered in splotches of fur but mostly wrinkled skin. It looked like that pussycat got in a fight with a lawnmower. The cat laid down and licked its paw for a moment before scratching its right ear. It was pierced with a small gold ring that bounced as it scratched.

I was so relieved it was just a cat, "Someone did a terrible job shaving their pussy! They should have gotten the bikini wax instead." I joked.

"And there it is!" a voice said and goosebumps rose on my skin, "Such a beautifully charming sense of humor from a lady." the voice snickered, "The beauty is in the crudity. Oh, how I've missed your lovely wit, Scarlet."

I looked at the cat, and it was still licking its paw. It tilted its head toward me with a strangely human expression. It couldn't have talked, right...

It opened its lips, bared its teeth, and gave me an actual smile, "Oh, I assure you, we are quite alone." it spoke, the cat spoke, "I just wanted to say, I really appreciate you taking notice in my fur. It's finally starting to grow back. You did quite the number on it the last time!"

Keep it together, Scarlet, you've seen weirder stuff on the net... mostly porn, "I'm sorry, do I know you, Cheshire? I'm fairly confident I didn't shave you. I have too much experience to do such a sloppy job."

He shook his head, "Yes and no, it's been a year. We get a fresh start so to speak. So, let's make the most of our time together."

Before I could say something, a doctor was suddenly before me wearing a porcelain rabbit mask. In his hand, he held a metal spike and a small hammer in the other. I tried to break free as he raised the spike to my eye, but I couldn't.

"No no no, stop!" I pleaded, "Let me go!"

"Don't worry, he's really good with his equipment. One good thrust and he'll send you to dreamland." Cheshire said with a dark smile.

I felt the sharp tip grazing my tear duct before he rammed the spike into my brain. The world crumbled, the ceiling cracked and disappeared into a void until only black remained...

"Ahhhhhhhhhh" I screamed as I awoke back on the floor of the padded room, "Bad kitty!" I yelled, "When I'm done with you, you're gonna be permanently bald!"

I ran my fingers over my eye, but there was no wound. It was like having an itch behind my eye I couldn't scratch. After a moment, I sighed in relief, but what the hell happened? There was nothing to defend myself with, also, I was still naked but not important. The psycho door left me alone the second time. The hallway was still dimly light, that hadn't changed.

I examined the hall and took a double take when I spotted a little girl in a white dress. She stood in the shadows holding my rabbit, but her face was obscured. She giggled and ran into a room, and I followed her. It was no place for a kid, she was in a lot of danger. The room beyond was pitch black inside, I couldn't see her.

"Little girl!" I called out in a hushed voice, "Little girl! Are you okay?" but no response came.

I wanted to go after her, but who knew what was in there. There was stupid, then there was running into a dark room in a place trying to kill you stupid. A tentacle came out of the darkness, I'd seen enough porn to know where this was going. It was warm and slimy as it wrapped around me, and I screamed when it dragged me in. I grabbed onto the doorway, but the crunching came.

Something was eating my legs, the only thing more horrific than the pain was my tearing flesh drowning out my screams. My muscles gave, it dragged into the darkness and splattered me across the floor. From the darkness, I awoke on the bus. Was it all a nightmare? Thank God it was over...

I heard, "No, love. This is a nightmare of your own making." and a man sitting in front of me rotated his head completely around, but he had Cheshire's head, "It will never be over!"

My heart skipped a beat, and I was suddenly back in the padded room. Crap, what was going on!? I rushed to my feet and out the door, and the lights were on this time. First, there was the matter of defending myself from the weirdness. A loose bar broken from a gurney would be my weapon. It wasn't the best, but it was better than getting into a catfight with my nails.

The moment I felt cocky came a loud scraping sound, it was metal being dragged. A man came around the corner of the hallway. He was tall with a ritualistic version of the porcelain mask, and a tidy pinstripe suit smoking a cigarette. He dragged a giant axe, like an executioner coming for my head. The sound of my bar rang down the hallway as I dropped it and ran.

"Too big, do not want!"

Shock struck me as I turned down the next hall to see no doors. As I turned back, I ducked in the nick of time to keep my head. How he caught up wasn't as important as finding a door. I scurried across the floor on my hands and feet until I could stand and run. Around every corner were endless, white halls, and a madman, ready to split me like wood.

Around the next corner was a hall that finally had a door. It was probably a trap, but I'd die if I didn't go through anyway. My heart throbbed in my chest and I could hear my bare feet slapping against the floor. The vibrations shooting up from my heels numbed my legs. Being chased by a murdering psychopath was really ruining streaking for me.

Blood rushed to my fingertips as I wildly swung my arms for all their worth. My lungs tightened as it got harder to breathe and my legs burned. The lights flickered out behind me like the darkness followed me. As I leaped forward, I grabbed the doorknob and crashed into the next room. The floor was wooden and made it hard to spin around after my roll.

It was gone, the door was gone, and in its place a wall. The place I found myself in was some kind of cabin or cottage. All around were dead bodies, and images of their slaughter flooded my head. In the confusion, I backed up, bumping against the wall. All the bodies hung from the ceiling by red threads, cutting through their throats.

My eyes widened, and I couldn't feel my body anymore. Through my throat was an axe, and my body fell lifelessly to the floor. The executioner removed his axe and my head rolled off the blade. Darkness encroached my sight, and as it faded, the girl in white walked into the room. In the darkness, I could feel my body, but something bound me.

I sat up on the floor of the padded room in a straight jacket. Still no pants, and stressed out of my mind without a way to calm the old nerves. The more I struggled against the jacket, the harder it tightened. Under different circumstances, I may have found it hot, but my hands were occupied.

The door slowly creaked open, "This is the place where your deepest fears took root."

Cheshire walked in with all his fur, but his left ear was pierced instead of his right.

"If I get a hold of you, I'm going to pound till you bleed!" I yelled.

"No." he calmly said, "I am the someone who's not the who you think I am. I am someone who you don't know you know yet."

"Some pussies are rotten, no matter how you shave and pierce them!" I said with snark.

"I am the key to your survival." he said, flinging a ring of keys into my lap with his tail.

The keys were cold and landed right on my sweet spot.

He turned back before he left, "These keys will set you free, they will open any door, but any door opened with these keys can never be locked again. Be careful what you wish for!" then he vanished into the darkness.

I stood up, dropping the keys to the floor, and hooked them with my toes, "My deepest fears, my tooshie! I've never seen this place before in my life. That cat must be stoned out his mind, or maybe I'm as batty as the cat..." I looked into the hallway or that was the plan.

Instead, there was a circular room with only doors staring back at me. Escaping was more important than counting them, one had to get me out, hopefully. I slowly stepped out of the padded room and moved toward the closest door. As I wobbled over, the keys jingled between my toes with each step. The floor was much warmer than before, my feet had become ice cold.

While I balanced on one foot, I tried the keys, until one drew my attention. Without knowing why, I tried it and the doorknob turned, but the door only opened a hair. I slammed it with my booty and it swung open, a gurney had been wedged against it. The gurney rattled as it rolled, and I heard it come to a stop as I struggled with the keys. They were in there pretty good, and my leg started to cramp as I tried to remove them.

They slipped out causing me to lose balance and fall to my butt. I dragged the keys with my toes, and moved farther into the room. The light from the doorway reflected off of anything shiny. I could make out a window, but the other side was pitch black. As I moved in closer, my reflection grew larger.

Looking through, I could only see my own image on the glass. Suddenly, there was a pain in my chest, and a light lit from the other side of the glass. A large operating room appeared below. I was stunned to see myself on an operating table cut open. All around were surgeons splitting me open from crotch to throat.

The pain grew worse, and blood stained the straight jacket mirroring the wound. At once, all the surgeons reached in and spread me open, my ribs broke and my flesh tore. My insides spilled out into the jacket, warming my skin. The pain was unimaginable, and before I could recover, they began slicing and dicing my organs. Every stroke of each blade was agony as they plucked out my insides.

I felt death come, but I wouldn't die, I was stuck in that moment.

"What, the pain too much for you?"

I looked down, gasping for air that would never come. One of the doctors turned to me and lowered his mask. It was Cheshire with a human body and cat head, grinning ear to ear.

He raised his scalpel, "And now, it's time to remove that beautiful pussy!" he began cutting again, only there was no pain, and after a moment, he lifted his cat form, "See what I did there?"

His cat self looked at me with a psychotic glare, "Finish it!" he grinned madly.

They went back to work and I blacked out from the pain. When I woke up, I was on the floor with a pain going down my body. I huffed, taking shallow breaths, I could breathe again but it hurt. Using the wall as a crutch, I inched my way to my feet. In my reflection, I saw the wound stitched up, stretching out the top and bottom of my jacket.

Pain surged through my head without warning, it felt like my brain was breaking. It was on fire, I couldn't think, and my body stumbled on its own. My toes wouldn't let go of the keys, I dragged them behind me without thinking. I moved back to the circular room, and another door was already open. When I wobbled to the door, I fell into it and pushed it open.

Inside, another me was strapped to a chair with some metal device to her head. She was being pumped full of electricity, I could feel my brain breaking. I tried to get her out of the chair, but there was nothing I could do without my arms. Her brain was frying and mine was going right along with hers. The switches were across the room, and tried flipping them with my head.

No matter how many I flipped, the current wouldn't stop. Soon, everything melted, burning up before my eyes. My brain was breaking down, it couldn't hold it together, and reality fell apart around me. My vision incinerated, like film melting away and left me to the darkness. When I woke up, I was on the floor and could barely move.

I got to my feet and noticed that she was missing from the chair. In the metal cabinet next to me, my reflection showed my hair burned and my scalp charred. Before I could figure anything out, a large, fat man burst into the room. He was dressed like a chef with a tall, white hat, and his apron was covered in blood and other various fluids. He screamed at me as he flipped the gurney, then charged me.

I was helpless as he descended upon me. He lifted me by my throat, I felt my neck twist as my head hit the ceiling. My kicks did nothing as he slammed me into the metal cabinet, knocked the wind out of me, and hurt my back. My jaw smacked down hard when he tossed me to the floor. I watched a few of my teeth bounce away as they flew out in a spray of blood.

When he lifted my head and slammed it into the floor, I was knocked out. The last thing I remembered was the feeling of my cheekbone cracking on the floor. I felt something cold sliding against my legs and bum, the headache and brain damage were the least of my problems. My vision was blurry at best, but I saw the hallway sliding away from me. I felt the grooves of the linoleum floor sliding under my butt and thighs as the chief dragged me down the hallway by my hair.

I drifted in and out but caught glimpses of what happened around me. Animals hanging from hooks and body parts strewn across the floor flashed before my eyes. There was a sudden thump as I was thrown down, only to realize I was on a butcher's block. He was going to kill me. My body wasn't healing like it was before, and I feared this time nothing would keep me from dying.

My arms were still bound, but it mattered little since I couldn't move. As I moaned and wiggled, I rolled my head back, and a knife popped into view. The chief had left the kitchen, it was my chance. I threw my hips around until I fell off the butcher's block. It was hard to move or breath, but I managed to inch forward a little at a time.

The counter seemed so far away, a goal impossible to reach. I pushed my face against the cabinet and smeared blood all over it. I used my neck to lift myself up, but it was a slow process. When I got to my knees, I rested my head on the counter and tried to breathe. Sounds came from the hallway, he was on his way back.

I rose up and shook like a leaf as I grabbed the knife with my mouth before I fell. No way I could cut the straps fast enough if I held it in my mouth. After I dropped it into my lap, and I positioned it between my knees. I moved my arms against the blade vigorously, constantly checking the door. The first sleeve tore freeing a hand, and I grabbed the knife.

The rest tore quickly, and I had a weapon. Just when I relaxed, he barged into the kitchen. He let out an ungodly roar and rushed me with a horrible expression of rage. Fear was an excellent motivator, my legs carried me away fast. I ran back to the hall, an endless maze of them.

I threw anything in his path to slow him down. He eventually fell over and ran to the only door. It was locked, then I realized I didn't have the ring of keys. He rose to his feet, and I was cornered. If I was going to fight, I needed to be able to move freely.

I dropped the knife and pulled on my straight jacket hard. It was on so tight, but I tugged on it with all my might. His stomps echoed down the hallway, and I panicked. It was now or never, and all my wiggling made it shift and come off. When it came off, my pain was gone, my wounds healed, and my hair returned.

My body felt good, a full range of motion was back at my fingertips. With the knife, I was ready to fight, but it changed before my eyes. From an old, dirty, kitchen knife came an ornate blade made of silver in a flash of light. I didn't question it, I was going to carve him like a honey glazed ham. He was moving in slow motion, and I slid around him, slicing his side along the way.

The rage inside consumed him and he flailed wildly. I weaved around, slashing him repeatedly, splattering his blood, and drenching myself. I was so fast I could see a trail of my own movements, it scared yet exhilarated me at the same time, but was a familiar feeling. I felled him and while he was on his knees, I slit his throat. In his death, the red blood glistened on my skin.

The door I had tried only moments earlier slowly creaked open. The door bashed against the wall as I came running through and found myself in a waiting room. With nothing left to stop me, I darted past the reception desk to the front doors. Outside, I had expected another trap to kill me, but there was nothing. It was night, and rain was pouring from the sky relentlessly.

I flew down the steps, but at the end of the stone pathway, I found only darkness. The land stretched off into nothingness, and just ended like an unfinished painting. The sky stretched beyond the horizon as the moon shone down on me.

I spun around to the building and saw a red, neon sign that read, "Cherry Hill Asylum".

If it was supposed to mean something, it was lost upon me, I'd never seen the place before.

"Crap! Nowhere to run." where the hell was I?

As I backed up, I bumped into something, "It may not be where it all started, but this place has come to house all your terrors. It's very important, it is where we first met after all."

As I spun, I was horrified to see that I was back inside the asylum, trapped in the center of a four-way intersection. At the four ends walked identical cat versions of Cheshire.

"Why are you so insistent on leaving?" they said in unison, "We still have so much fun to have!"

They leaned forward as if stretching and dug their claws into the floor. They tore through the floor as they pulled them back. Their bodies began to twist and deform. Bone spikes popped off their spines, and their skin sucked under their ribs. Their teeth became razors, claws like blades, and eyes pitch black.

Before they were cats, now the size of lions and twisted like demons. They rushed, and I was trapped me between them. My back was against the wall, the corner touching me down my spine. The doors were gone, and I was screwed.

What was going to happen when I died this time?

"I don't know about you..." it was Cheshire, the other one with the pierced left ear, "but I'll be leaving."

Then the wall I was pressed against disappeared and caused me to fall into a dark void. I fell until I stopped without landing. There was nothing to stand on, but I stood. I patted my body down to make sure I was still in one piece when I came to a horrifying realization. My boobies were gone, it was a full, level five emergency, oh the horror!

I screamed out, but my voice, I sounded like a little girl, and I wore an old, torn dress. I could suddenly feel the dirt beneath my feet and crouched down. I ran my fingers across the ground and searched for anything. There was a crackling sound that echoed softly at first but became louder. A burning light flashed before me, and I was blinded.

I reached around frantically to keep from falling and found a wooden bar. With both hands, I grabbed onto it to pull myself up, but I couldn't let go. My hands were bound, a rope ground against my wrists. When the light faded, there was a village gone mad. They screamed and waved torches as they huddled around a fire.

Upon the flames were a man and a woman burning alive. Next to me were others, we were lined up, next to be sent to the stake. No amount of struggle could free me from my bindings.

"You're next." a familiar voice said, it was the bad Cheshire, "What will you do?" he asked.

At his feet, sat a saw, then he walked away. I reached out with my foot as I tried to grab the saw with my toes. Once it was hooked it, I used my feet to saw the ropes. It hurt, the saw cut my wrists, but there was nothing to be gained from stopping. If I didn't fight past the pain and blood, I'd burn alive.

I clenched my eyelids closed tightly, and when they opened I was on a bus. It was a run-down bus, a piece of junk, but more surprising was the piece of rusty metal in my hands. My wrist was bleeding, I was cutting into it with the metal. Everything was hazy, I couldn't focus or think. My legs began running beneath me as my lungs gasped for air.

By the time I had my wits about me, I was on top of a man. My mouth inches from his, and he was shaking wildly. I'd become a rapist or so I had thought until a green energy flowed from his mouth and into mine. I was baring my teeth, as if ready to bite him like a wild animal. As soon as I realized what was happening, I jumped off the man.

I freaked out! What had I done to him, and what was that green energy? As I paced back and forth, I drilled myself with an unending stream of questions. I noticed my wrist, the wound was smaller than before. It looked nearly healed.

"What's going on!?" I was still freaking out.

In the distance, was the rusted bus, I was in the graveyard. All around the rain was pouring, and my legs and hands were covered in mud. I looked down at the man I had attacked as he lay flat on the ground. I squatted next to him and tapped his face, which was cold to the touch.

"Hey!" I said loudly, "Are you okay? Hello!"

He was groggy, "I can... see your panties." he said with a smile.

"Oh thank God, he lives!" I grinned.

I dragged him to a tombstone and leaned him up against it. After taking my backpack off, I did what any self-respecting woman should have done and thanked my knight with a pair of my undies on his head.

I pinched his cheek, "There you go, big boy! Sweet dreams!"

"Uh-huh... yeah... okay.." then he fell asleep.

Hopefully, he'd be okay and not get sick from the rain. As I walked away, I zipped my backpack when I realized my rabbit was gone. Hysterical was an understatement, where was it, where was my rabbit!? My thoughts were jumbled, I was becoming frantic. I was about to lose it.

"The bus!" I said before I ran.

My feet sloshed through the rain-soaked ground as I ran to the bus. It was farther away than I thought, it felt much closer when I ran in the haze. Upon reaching the bus, I stormed to the back seat. My rabbit was on the floor in front of it. A deep fear sank into my gut as I grabbed a hold of it.

I curled up with my rabbit and rocked back and forth as it calmed me. If I had lost it, I don't know what I would have done. The fear of losing it was too much for me to process. I had been so caught up in being afraid that it took a moment to notice. Next to me was the ornate, silver blade resting on the opposite seat...

CHAPTER 24
SYN INCARNATE

CLEARCREST, THE 27TH -- The Hot Head and the Boy sat in an awkward silence.

It had been nearly fifteen minutes since I woke the kid, but he wouldn't speak. He just sat there all pissed off.

"You know, kid, I didn't have to make sure you were okay. After you attacked me, I could have killed you, and you'd have never known."

"I didn't ask for your help, and I don't want it!" he snapped at me.

"Sweet Jesus! I would've bet money you were mute." then I sighed.

"Let me go…" he said.

"I'm not holding you hostage, you can leave." I doubt he'd believe me, "Is that what you've been so pissed about?"

He looked at me, the first direct eye contact he'd given, "So I can go, just like that?"

"Yep..." I stood, "I was making sure you weren't hurt. You know, when you bashed your head into the wall after hitting me in the tit, like a prick."

"I, umm... I no... I mean you... uh..." he fumbled his words.

"Are you always like that, or is it the head trauma?"

"My head hurts, but I'm fine." he said timidly, "And sorry for hitting you."

"By the way, where'd you get that coat."

"Some big..." he seemed confused why I would ask.

I cut him off, "Guy like ten feet tall that looked like he was cut from stone?"

He was shocked, "How'd you know!?"

I mumbled, "That dumbass would give his last leg to peg-legged pirate."

"What...?" I was confusing him.

"Oh, it's nothing..." I changed the subject, "Let me ask. Why aren't you locked up inside like everyone else?"

He was hesitant, "I'm looking for someone."

"They must be pretty important to risk your life."
He clenched his fists, "Yes, they are." he began shaking, "I'll do whatever it takes to find her." he shouted.

"Oh, so it's a girl!" I said.

He let it slip, "Yes..." he shied away, "She's my sister, and she's in trouble."

"What kind of trouble?" I asked and I saw the fire in his eyes.

"After that damn explosion at the airport, someone jumped us and did this to me!" he showed me the wound on his neck.

I stood in shock, "That's an electrical burn in the shape of a handprint, a Sleeper." I walked to him, "Your sister is in real trouble!" I crouched to look him in the eye, and placed my hand on his shoulder, "I don't believe in coincidences. Do you know a man named Chris?"

"How'd you know?" he was surprised.

"Damn!" I yelled, "This isn't good, he's going to be pissed." I pulled out my phone, "I have to call him." but my phone wouldn't work, "What do you mean no signal!?" I said as I smacked the damn thing.

"Lady!" the kid screamed.

"What the hell do you want, kid... Oh..." I realized what was going on, "So, that's why."

A fog was rolling in, the kid had probably thought the Sleeper was back. I, on the other hand knew it was her. The fog came in low, very thick, and maybe a foot high. Lights blinked out in the distance and followed the fog.

"What's happening? Why won't the phone work?" the kid was panicked.

"For the phone to work we'd need a cell tower, and we're not on earth anymore." I told him.

I don't know if he believed me, hell, I barely believe me, but it was the truth. There were more things out there I had been blind to all my life, like superpowers, demons, and the monsters in the night. I still hoped I'd wake from the nightmare, or maybe I'd gone crazy. For now, I was in her dimension, but I didn't know what she wanted.

The kid shouted, "What do you mean we're not on Earth anymore?"

"Kid, your brain will hurt less if I don't tell you." I replied, "But we're safe, unless you're asthmatic. Just look for a shop." then the last light faded, and we were left in complete darkness.

"What shop?"

A light shone from behind us, "That one!"

I turned to see the shop exactly as I had remembered it from the last time I had been there. It was an old building floating in black nothingness with fog drifting around it. The shop was a challenge to describe, there was no single theme, but it had style. Torches provided light, and decorations from every culture throughout the ages piled up around it. Mounted atop was a sign that read, "Faith's Guidance."

I stepped forward and pushed the cloth door aside, which made the beads beyond it rattle. Inside it smelled of smoke and incense, but that was a nice change from the odor of the city slums. Beyond was a massive collection of antiques that made the place a maze. I was pretty sure she was a hoarder. Like the outside, the antiques that filled the place were multicultural.

"Listen kid, don't touch anything." I said quietly.

"The name is Yuri, not kid!" he was growing some balls.

I rolled my eyes, "If you haven't hit puberty, you're still a kid. Don't touch anything if you want to live that long because half this shit will kill you!"

"And the other half?" he was being a smart-ass.

"Kill you slower..." a woman's voice said.

"Madame Flora!"

We entered a cleared area, and in the center was a chair, or was it a throne. Floating above it was a little old lady sitting on a levitating pillow. The throne sat atop a structure with stairs that had a red runner down the center. All along the sides were cloth murals on them, candles, and incense. She flicked her cigarette holder and dropped the ash on the floor.

My grandmother had one, and they always reminded me of a pipe for women.

"So, you couldn't get off the throne to greet us?" I said, popping an attitude.

"Hello, woman with the mouth of a sailor." she mocked me, "Do not touch!" she suddenly shouted.

It wasn't me, so I look back at the boy who had an innocent expression on his face. As with all kids, it was too innocent, I could see right through him.

"The fuck, dude!?" I said as I smacked him upside the back of the head.

"Do not touch that potion, Yuri..." Madam flora continued, "It is intended for women, a failure. A strange side effect in men, testicles sprout from chin... Precisely three." and she held up her fingers equal to the count.

That was a mental image I didn't need, "What do you want, hag?" but she cut me off.

"I'm getting to that, loud mouth. Why must you always interrupt?" she shook her head, "Listen carefully, I will not repeat myself! Soon, the three kings of darkness will descend upon this world, two have risen, one shall reign. They will be drawn to fight one another, and no matter which wins, the war of kings will still come. I have seen all outcomes, but this cycle will end at the hands of the Starkiller.

"What the hell does that mean!?" I snapped, "Not a damn bit of that made any sense!"

"Well..." Yuri butted in, "Prophecies aren't supposed to make sense until the time comes. Simply knowing would change the order of events, making none of what you've been told of any use, because everything would have changed."

"Godslayer, you're smarter than the loud-mouthed ape!" the old bitch said.

"Oh, so you want some of this, you old hag!?" I snarled.

As I stomped toward her, she blew smoke in my face, and we were back in Clearcrest.

"Damn! I hate that woman." I clenched my fists.

"I know, right?" a man's voice said, "So long-winded and rude to boot! I once asked her how I could take over the world and she laughed. It was insensitive. My feelings were genuinely hurt."

I followed the voice to see a man sitting at the edge of a building. There was something evil about him, and it crushed my gut. Looking at him was like looking upon that man's darkness. He was dressed in a black trench coat with a hood covering all but his twisted smile. I recognize the outfit, he was with Umbrage.

"What the fuck does Umbrage want!?" I yelled.

"Straight to the point, I like that about you, Keira!" he stood, with his arms held out wide and proclaimed, "Syn Incarnate at your service, and I, little miss am the man who's going to open the Gates of Hell! There's more to it, but I'll make a slideshow when everyone's together. I will, however, open the floor to questions, though." then pointed to Yuri, "Yes, the kid with his hand up!"

"Are you high?" Yuri asked.

"On life, yes!" he said, breathing deeply through his nose, "Thanks for asking! Now, with our Q&A session drawing to an end." a deranged look took over his eyes, "Where is Zero Heal!?"

The name ignited a fire inside me, and I lost control. Everything around me froze as power flowed into me, and my rage exploded into a vicious flame that encased my body. I gathered it in my hand and threw it at him, but he easily evaded. Hitting him wasn't the goal, it was a distraction.

"I never want to hear that name again!!!" I screamed as I leaped and swung a car at him like a bat.

"That's the spirit! Now tell me where he is!" his sadistic smile was just like his.

He evaded again, leaving my feet against the building as I clung to the car which was barely balancing on the edge. One false move, I'd fall and be crushed, but I had to beat the motherfucker's face in. Before I could make my move, he raised his hand, then came the darkness. I couldn't let it touch me, so I threw myself onto the street. I couldn't believe what I saw, but I thought only Zero could that.

Darkness came from his hand like it was nothing, but it shouldn't have. Umbrage themselves said humans weren't able to manipulate the main three forces of the universe, Darkness, Light, and None. Syn and Zero, I was sure that the two of them weren't human. Either way, it left me in a bad spot, any matter touched was corrupted and twisted by it. The darkness he released shot forth like a flame, but hit like bricks. The car slid across the edge and smashed down onto the ground. The black flame disintegrated most of the metal, and released what looked like dark blue snow that floated up. What wasn't eroded was infected, like the darkness was a disease.

"How did you do that!?" I screamed, "What are you?"

"I see you're starting to figure it out." he sounded satisfied, "Now, I'm a pretty smart guy, so I know you're going to need a little more motivation to give him up."

"I don't know where he is..." I snapped, "and I hope he's fucking dead!"

"If you honestly don't know where he is, then you better find him..." he smiled, "and you better hope he's alive."

"If I had to choose between you, and that monster, I'd put my foot up your ass. You don't want a monster like him to be alive."

"Oh, but I do, and here's why you should too!" he said as he held his hands out.

The ground shook, rumbled, and ripped like paper beneath him. A crack formed and spread down the street. From it rushed a black liquid that rose like a geyser, Darkwater! The most dangerous thing on this wretched planet and he had gotten it past the Hellgate. Despite the impossibility of such a thing, I was prepared to run for my life.

A drop of Darkwater destroyed the world, creating monsters and worst of all, Sleepers. Before I could run, I noticed it wasn't rushing out. Instead, it continued to rise, he was controlling it. That was something not even that bastard could do, so this guy made it to second place on my shit list. I had to stop him fast, before he spread the infection, or was it too late?

It stopped and inside floated a large, black crystal. I saw something inside, a long strand of blonde hair. As I moved closer, a woman's face became visible, no, it was a little girl.

"This, this is why you're going to help me!" he smirked evilly.

"Yeah... Never seen her before."

"No, but he has! " and he pointed to Yuri.

Yuri's face was twisted in horror as he held his hands toward her, "Sis!" he screamed with tears, "What have you done, you've turned her into one of those monsters!?"

"Don't be a drama queen! I've entombed her in darkness, she's perfectly safe I assure you, and I'll return her as good as new if everyone plays their part in my little game."

"Why would you take his sister? They don't have anything to do with this?"

"It has everything to do with him." then he shrugged, "Just not for years."

It was ludicrous, "And you think this is going to make me help you now!?"

A small smile creaked across his face like stepping on a floorboard on a dark night, "Everyone has someone they hold dear, what makes you think you're any different? Mwahahahaha."

I was filled with fear, anger, and despair, "No..."

"Yes!" he said with a devious smile, "This was just a display of my power. If you need another, why not try this one!" he said as he held up his hands.

His fingers stretched out, and gripped down like he crushed something. Suddenly, the Hellgate protecting the city shattered like glass. He destroyed the only thing keeping the Abyss at bay. We were defenseless against the other monsters born of the Darkwater. The rotten odor of the outside world rode in on the wind like a plague.

The black crystal and the Darkwater sucked back into the ground. With a sick smile, he vanished into a cloud of black smoke. I stared in shock as the city went to hell around me...

CHAPTER 25
AGAINST THE ABYSS

CLEARCREST, THE 27TH -- Keira and Yuri were left in astonishment as the Abyss consumed the city. Syn had the power to create a new world order.

The city was riddled with chaos, but it sounded quiet, even if it was dead all the same. I couldn't help but freeze in awe of such power. No creature of the Abyss or Sleeper had ever left a mark on a Hellgate before. The arrival of this mysterious man was sure to usher in a new era just as the Hellgates had before him. There was nothing we could do but wait and die.

I felt the ground as it shook repetitively. It was all too familiar, it foreshadowed of the Abyss. With each stomp, my rage grew, festered, and ate away at me like a disease. That man had crossed the line and fucked with the wrong bitch. Everyone thought they could fuck with me, and it pissed me off.

Then the perfect punching bags lined up for me, they could feel my rising power. First, was a Croag, a twenty-foot tall beast similar to a caveman crossed with an ogre. In the distance, I saw a Vetril, a large, flying, multi-fallen collection of rotting flesh in the shape of a bird. Lastly, I could hear an Apor as it slithered in the distance, a snakelike melding of bone that could swallow a bus whole. These three were some of the worst heavy hitters the Abyss had to offer.

They were probably all over the city by now, killing hundreds of people a minute. It was all that bastard's fault. My rage boiled my blood, and steam rose off me as my skin evaporated the moisture in the air. My muscles grew larger with every breath and tightened back down. Power flooded me, my blood ran like magma, and my skin burned like desert sands.

When every cell of my being infused with my power, I changed. My body became like fire, and my hair became light as air. From the roots, an orange glow flowed through each strand. Embers jumped off my hair as if it were a flame. I was ready to bust some heads.

It had been a year since I had fought one of them, they'd be a good test to gauge how much I had grown!

"Time to die, you disgusting fucknuts!" I shouted as I jumped forward.

The Croag was the only one who had found me, and it swung a club at me or was it a tree. I dealt with it like I would have anything else, I shattered it to fucking pieces with my fist. I whipped my leg at its face and it stumbled into the side of a building. As rubble fell, I turned to the Apor that had joined the fight. As it lunged, I rolled to the side, and I dug my fingers into its bones.

They were hard as the devil was slick, and I could feel my nails tearing. When I finally got a grip, I dug my feet into the ground as it dragged me. Asphalt piled up before me as we stopped. Wasting no time, I heaved its tail over my shoulder, and pulled with everything I had. I whipped it around, bringing down the front of a building before I let it fly into the distance.

"Take that, you motherfucker!" I said as I bit a piece of nail hanging from a bloody finger, and spit it out as the big guy got up, "Ready for round two, huh!? Okay, I got just the thing for you." I ran to the rubble, and tore it like cardboard until I had what I needed, "Okay asshole! Let's rumble!"

From the pile next to me, I kicked up a wooden beam. It spun in the air and with a timed punch, I aimed at the Croag. My punch was off, and it zoomed by it. If you can't hit a target, hit everything, and I unleashed a volley of beams. The second, third, and fourth missed, or winged him, but the fifth hit.

It was in the shoulder, no good, so I launched more, as many as I had. My lucky shot stabbed him in the left eye, and I had my kill in the bag. As it tried to pull the beam out, I leaped in for my final attack. My fist slammed into the beam and drove out the back of its skull. I didn't bask in my victory because the Apor had come back.

Its hard exterior made it impossible for me to hurt from the outside, there was only one thing I could do. I drew in power from my surroundings, and ice formed where the energy had left. The timing had to be exact or I was dead, but a horrible shrill rang my ears. The energy, I'd been careless and let so much gather it had put me on its radar. The Vetril's attention had shifted to me, and I was trapped between two things that wanted to eat me alive.

It swooped down and left me to be bird food or snake grub. Fuck options, I jumped out of the way, and let the Vetril clutch the Apor in its talons. The two struggled and with them occupied, I had my chance to run. With the Abyss coming, I had to leave the city, but first I had to get to my father. I ran for my bike with my heart pounding against my chest, and that's when I saw the kid.

He was frozen in fear, couldn't blame him, but I couldn't leave him either.

As soon as I got close, he pulled a gun on me, "Stay back, you monster!" he screamed.

His entire body was violently shaking, "Put the gun down, kid. We have to get out of here."

"I'm not going anywhere with you!" and he crawled away in terror.

"Shoot the monster, you'll be doing the world a favor. Oh and good luck using YOUR superpowers to kill the things that want to eat you, alive." then he looked between us thinking, "You want to survive, but you want to save your sister more? If you think you can do it on your own, give it your all. Me, on the other hand, I'm getting the hell out of dodge before my ass gets eaten." and I backed away, "Whether you join me or not is up to you."

I started the bike and looked back as the kid watched the fallen fight, "Do you know where that bastard is!?" he shouted.

"No, but I do know where he's going to be, and I'm putting my fist through his skull."

He kept his gun pointed at me as he moved closer, "I don't trust you, but I want my sister back."

I snatched the gun from him and slid it under my belt. The look on his face, I had broken what little trust he had. "You'll get it back, I just didn't want you shooting me after we hit the first bump." and he backed off.

I heard a god-awful shriek from the Vetril, it had been injured and fled. The Apor, on the other hand, had turned its attention back to us, and it looked hungry.

"Times up, kid, decide!" I told him, "Live or die!?"

He grit his teeth before he jumped on the bike and wrapped his arms around me. I put the pedal to the metal and shot out of there like a bat out of hell. The Apor crashed into the side of a building as it turned after us. It was going to catch up, it was only a matter of time. All I had to do was get some ground on it, and I could finish the damn snake off.

My original plan would still work, but I needed the time to charge up. I took the back alleys to slow it down so we could gain some distance. I weaved through them as it crashed behind us, and it couldn't follow. As I glanced into the mirror, I saw it take to the rooftops. I had gained a second or two at the most.

I had to step up my game and make a ballsy move if I wanted to get out alive. My rage was heating me up, and I meant literally burning. The grips of my handlebar we're starting to melt, and I can only imagine what the kid felt. Getting too hot was bad, I needed to calm down or we'd die. As I tried to calm down, I strained my brain trying to think of something.

I saw the perfect way to end it once and for all. I turned toward a building low to the ground with nothing but glass on the bottom floor. I jumped the curb and drove through as glass shards cut me. The dumb beast followed, but the building crumbled down on top of it as planned. In the mirror, I saw it thrashing around as it tried to wiggle its way in.

After a couple of blocks, I came to a stop and jumped off the bike. It was time to finish what I started with that damn snake.

"What the hell are you doing, it's going to catch us." Yuri shouted.

I pointed to him, "Shut it!"

After taking a deep breath, I began pulling in energy. Ice spread out and slowly encroached upon the ground. The Apor showed its ugly face as it threw rubble into the air. It was my chance to end it or die trying, just the way I liked it. As it came at me, I trust my hands forward and released all the energy I had gathered.

It opened its mouth to eat me, and all the energy went down its throat. That split second was all I needed to burn the fucker to nothing more than ash as it bones bounced down the street. The gust of wind that followed stirred the ashes, and they danced away on the breeze. It was a shame, I could have made some nice snakeskin boots.

"Shit!" I was wasting time that could have been spent beating that prick's face in. The two of us sped off on the bike, and my phone rang.

I didn't have the time for that shit, "What!?" I shouted without checking the caller ID.

"What the hell's going on out there!? The Hellgate is gone, we need to escape the city!" I recognized that blockhead Vincent's voice.

"That bastard going after my dad!" I yelled.

"Wait, who's going after your dad? Wait, where you are, I'm coming to help you!"

"That bastard's looking for your brother!" I told him, "He's not going to wait."

"Shit, you're going to need my help! Just wait for me, please!" he begged.

"This is personal!" and I dropped the phone on the street.

The only one who was going to beat his face in was me, but driving against the flow of people was slowing me down. I broke away from the crowd and took the back way. It was smooth sailing to my dad's casino, even if it was the long way. By the time I got there, the parking lot was empty. I had no idea if he had made it out in time, or if that bastard had gotten him.

It didn't matter anyway, the ground rumbled, and it was all over for us. They asphalt split, and through the cracks rushed Darkwater. Again, it was happening, the Darkwater would consume everything. We were sucked under the black wave of water and everything faded. There wasn't a single thing to feel, just an unending emptiness that enveloped me.

I slipped into the black void for a second time. Was that really how it was going to end...

CHAPTER 26
THE GAME HAS ONLY JUST BEGUN

SYN'S LAIR -- The Ghost loomed at Syn's side with a blade behind her back.

Syn had begun his game, and he was more than pleased with himself. He disgusted me, but I was forced to be by his side. The walls were bare except for long red curtains spaced out evenly along them. I stood as far from him as I could as he rested in his tacky throne. I wanted to use my blade, slit his throat, and feast on his innards.

Then a knock came at the throne room door, "Yes, come in." Syn said as he kicked his legs up onto the arm of the throne.

The door opened, and HE came in. Wearing that ridiculous crow mask and his Victorian-era suit. I may have wanted to break every bone in his body and skin him, but he had more taste than the shit bastard we served. He walked in carrying a small hand mirror. It was intriguing, and I watched it along his entire journey across the room.

He bowed as the disinterested Syn picked at his fingernails, "Lord Syn, I have found it!"

Syn kicked his legs to the floor and gripped his throne with both hands, "Really!?" he said like an eager child.

"Truly, sir. It was no small task, but I have." he said, holding up the mirror.

Upon its reflection was the image of a ring, and I was struck with terror by what I felt coming from within it. I stumbled back in horror as my legs failed to work. My cloak caught under my foot and I tripped. On the floor, I crawled away until I hit the wall. I clung to the curtains as I pushed my feet against the floor, hoping I would go through the wall.

Syn turned to me with a smug look on his face, "Ah, so you can feel it, can't you, girlie? Now, you see, that is the proper reaction to this ring."

He could feel it too, and he was happy about it!? What kind of mad would a person have to be to be thrilled by the twisted darkness coming from that ring?

He looked away from me, "Good, Magnus! With the game underway and the ring found, I can move forward onto the fourth phase of my plan without any worry. Soon, the towers will rise, and we will be one step closer to our goal."

"And the girl?" Magnus said as he looked my way, "Is she serving you well, Lord Syn?

"She has some rebellious spunk in her. Every now and again I catch her looking at my throat like it's a chew toy, but she has her uses." he said while he gestured for the mirror, "Now, leave us girl, or I'll lock you in a cage with this ring when we finally get it!"

My legs shook violently at the thought, and I ran as Magnus passed the mirror to Syn.

I heard Syn say one last thing before they became inaudible, "With any luck, the goddess will return from the moon in the near future. With her power, the true game will begin...

EPILOGUE
SOME MONSTERS ARE BORN

CHAPTER 0 CONTINUED -- The mysterious man's uncertainty made him defensive when I raised my hand like a gun. I opened my mouth and clicked my tongue as I dropped my thumb like the hammer. Then I silently made the lip motions for the word bang as a beam of light shot from my finger and past him into the distance. The beam shined like a spider's web in the moonlight and vanished. For a moment there was nothing, then an explosion tossed up sand.

He ran when I smiled and fired my second shot farther off than the first. He launched a volley of fireballs as I adjusted to my new found power. Either I was cocky or didn't care when I ran into the fireballs and swatted them away like flies. I closed the distance, locked hands with him, and bashed his face with my forehead. His hands lit on fire in a desperate attempt to break free.

I fought through the pain as I kneed his gut and head-butted again. He broke free, but my hand remained on fire. My hands exploded furiously and formed fire of their own. I slapped my hands together to release a pillar of flame. It spun forward, threw up sand, and melted it into a glass rib cage.

The pillar hit hard, but he remained on his feet. As the flames disappeared, I vanished from sight in an instant. Suddenly, I was in front of him with a wicked smile and a fist full of pain. When I punched, the glass shattered into dust and flew past us. He was thrown back but refused to fall.

I raised both hands like guns and fired beams of light as we ran parallel to one another. Light danced in the sky as we fought, but I suddenly stopped in my tracks as my eyes went red.

He stopped and waited, "Do you feel that...?" I asked as my white hair reverted to brown, and my jacket exploded into light particles.

I looked up and saw the end of the world riding on the back of a massive flaming rock burning in the atmosphere. I fell to my knees, there was nowhere to run or hide. It dropped behind a mass of lights in the distance. There was nothing at first, but we were rocked by an explosion. A storm of sand rolled across the desert like a tsunami. It swallowed everything, it was over, it was the beginning of the end... -- NEVADA, SEPTEMBER 2ND, 2006 - THE NIGHT OF THE EVENT

TO BE CONTINUED…

In Vol: 2

ABOUT THE AUTHOR

Michael Anderson, a man who grew up with one thing on his mind, big swords, fight scenes, giant explosions, and epic one-liners. Unfortunately, he got nowhere in life and had friends who refused to publicly acknowledge his existence, the end. At least he could always count on himself to laugh at his lame jokes...